William Shakespeare's The Comedy of Errors: A Retelling in Prose

David Bruce

Published by David Bruce, 2022.

This is a work of fiction. Similarities to real people, places, or events are entirely coincidental.

WILLIAM SHAKESPEARE'S THE COMEDY OF ERRORS: A RETELLING IN PROSE

First edition. July 23, 2022.

Copyright © 2022 David Bruce.

ISBN: 979-8201122379

Written by David Bruce.

Table of Contents

CAST OF CHARACTERS...1
CHAPTER 1 2
CHAPTER 2 11
CHAPTER 3 25
CHAPTER 4 39
CHAPTER 5 61
APPENDIX A: ABOUT THE AUTHOR...................................78
APPENDIX B: SOME BOOKS BY DAVID BRUCE 79

Dedication

Dedicated to My Brother Frank

Frank was reluctant to write the words below, but he did at my request because it's an opportunity to show that people still do good deeds. This can help restore people's faith in humanity.

"I've put some thought into this, and here a few Good Deeds I've done.

"I've bought breakfast more than once for complete strangers at my favorite local diner (Tommy's Diner) just because they looked like they could use a free meal.

"A woman came into Tommy's Diner, looking like she could use a decent meal and would appreciate it being free. I watched as she walked through the restaurant and sat down. I thought to myself, 'Buy her lunch.' I fought the urge and told myself no. I looked at her after she ordered and received her meal and thought to myself, 'Buy her lunch.' Again, I told myself no. She is a complete stranger, and money is hard to come by for me as well as everyone else. I was in line at the check-out waiting to pay my bill. She came up and got into line behind me and I thought to myself, 'Buy her lunch!' I looked at her, she looked at me, I reached out and grabbed her ticket, but she didn't want to let go. I told her sort of sternly, 'I don't know why, but I really, really want to pay for your lunch. I know we are complete strangers, but I feel like I am supposed to pay for your lunch. Will you please give me the pleasure of paying for this?' She almost cried, but she did allow me the pleasure.

"In Columbus, Ohio, almost always someone is at the gas station wanting money. One day this guy asked for money. I asked him, 'Why do you want money?' He said he's hungry. (If you don't know, Speedway has hotdogs and other food and drink items.) I said, 'Come inside, I'll buy you something to eat.' He was a really nice guy. His name was Dave, and he was an Army veteran; he may have been a little mentally ill after serving in the military. He talked to me about the war (don't know what war) and how he was over there fighting bulldozers. I think a couple of hotdogs and a hot coffee made his day. It really put a smile on his face. I ended up liking this guy and I'd look for him when I was getting gas so I could help him out.

"One time a guy came in the restaurant selling an old leather jacket for $10.00 so he could get some gas. It didn't fit me, and I didn't want it anyway, but I bought it and then donated the jacket.

"A woman was driving her car with the alarm going off, so I helped her figure out how to turn it off. She had the key fob, so I'm sure she didn't steal the car.

"These are a few of the good deeds I've had the pleasure of doing."

Educate Yourself
Read Like A Wolf Eats
Be Excellent to Each Other
Books Then, Books Now, Books Forever

***

Do you know a language other than English? If you do, I give you permission to translate this book, copyright your translation, publish or self-publish it, and keep all the royalties for yourself. (Do give me credit, of course, for the original retelling.)

I would like to see my retellings of classic literature used in schools, so I give permission to the country of Finland (and all other countries) to give copies of this book to all students forever. I also give permission to the state of Texas (and all other states) to give copies of this book to all students forever. I also give permission to all teachers to give copies of this book to all students forever.

Teachers need not actually teach my retellings. Teachers are welcome to give students copies of my eBooks as background material. For example, if they are teaching Homer's *Iliad* and *Odyssey*, teachers are welcome to give students copies of my *Virgil's Aeneid: A Retelling in Prose* and tell students, "Here's another ancient epic you may want to read in your spare time."

CAST OF CHARACTERS

SOLINUS: Duke of Ephesus, an ancient Greek town on the coast of Ionia in what is now Turkey.

EGEON: a merchant of Syracuse, a town in Sicily.

ANTIPHOLUS OF EPHESUS and ANTIPHOLUS OF SYRACUSE: twin brothers, and sons to EGEON and EMILIA.

DROMIO OF EPHESUS and DROMIO OF SYRACUSE: twin brothers, and slaves of the two ANTIPHOLUSES.

BALTHAZAR: a merchant.

ANGELO: a goldsmith.

FIRST MERCHANT: friend to Antipholus of Syracuse.

SECOND MERCHANT: to whom Angelo is a debtor.

PINCH: a schoolmaster and would-be exorcist.

EMILIA: wife to Egeon; an Abbess at Ephesus.

ADRIANA: wife to Antipholus of Ephesus.

LUCIANA: Adriana's sister.

LUCE: Kitchen maid to Adriana.

A Courtesan.

Jailer, Officers, Attendants.

SCENE: Ephesus.

Epidamnus: a town on the eastern shore of the Adriatic Sea between the Italian Peninsula and the Balkan Peninsula.

Epidaurus: a town in Greece at the Saronic Gulf.

The Porcupine: name of the house where the courtesan lives.

The Phoenix: name of the house where Antipholus of Ephesus and Adriana live.

The Centaur Inn: name of the inn where Antipholus of Syracuse and Dromio of Syracuse stay.

Marks, ducats, angels: units of money.

CHAPTER 1

— 1.1 —

In a hall in the palace of Solinus, the Duke of Ephesus, Egeon, a merchant of Syracuse, had been sentenced to death unless he could raise a thousand marks to ransom himself. Present were Duke Solinus, Egeon, a jailer, and some police officers and attendants.

Egeon said, "Proceed, Solinus, and kill me. Dying will end all my woes."

The Duke of Ephesus replied, "Merchant of Syracuse, plead no more."

Egeon thought, *If the Duke of Ephesus considers what I just said to be pleading for my life, he must have a guilty conscience. Apparently, he does not like the law that he feels obligated to enforce.*

The Duke of Ephesus continued, "I am not inclined to bend our laws and avoid enforcing them. The enmity and discord that of late has sprung from the rancorous outrage of your Duke of Syracuse to our merchants, who are fair-dealing countrymen of Ephesus, who lacked the money to ransom their lives and therefore paid with their blood his penalty that came from enforcement of his rigorous statutes, ensure that I will allow no pity to replace my threatening looks.

"Because of the deadly quarrels between your seditious countrymen and our citizens of Ephesus, the governments of Ephesus and of Syracuse have forbid by law any traffic or trade between these two cities. Indeed, the penalty for disobeying these laws is severe. If anyone born at Ephesus is seen at any markets and fairs in Syracuse, he will die and his possessions will be forfeited to the Duke of Syracuse unless he can raise a thousand marks to pay the penalty for breaking the law and so save his life. The same is true if anyone born at Syracuse is seen at any markets and fairs in Ephesus.

"Your possessions, valued at the highest rate, are not worth even a hundred marks, and therefore by law you are condemned to die by beheading before the Sun sets."

"Still, I have this comfort," Egeon said. "When I die with the evening Sun, all my woes shall end and be done."

"Well, merchant of Syracuse," the Duke of Ephesus said, "tell us briefly the cause for your leaving your native home in Syracuse and the reason why you came to Ephesus."

Egeon said, "You could not have given me a heavier task than to tell you my griefs, which are unspeakable. Yet, so that the world may witness that my capital punishment has come about because of natural affection and not because of a vile offence, I will tell you about my sorrows. I was born in Syracuse, and I wed a woman who was fortunate except that she married me, but I could have made her happy except that our luck was bad. With her I lived in joy; our wealth increased because of the prosperous voyages that I often made to Epidamnus, a town on the eastern shore of the Adriatic Sea.

"Unfortunately, my agent in Epidamnus died there and I needed to take care of the goods that were then left untended. I left my wife at Syracuse and sailed to Epidamnus. We were separated and lacked our usual kind embracings for almost six months, but my wife, almost fainting because of the pleasing punishment that women bear — pregnancy — voyaged to join me at Epidamnus,

"She had not been long there before she became the joyful mother of two good sons — identical twins so alike that they could not be distinguished except by their names. That very hour, and in the same inn, a woman of a low social class was delivered of a similar burden; she gave birth to male twins, both identical. I bought those boys — their parents were very poor — and I brought them up to serve my sons.

"My wife, considerably proud of her two sons, daily asked me to take our family back to our home in Syracuse. Reluctantly, I agreed. This was unfortunate. Too soon, we went aboard a ship. We had sailed only a league — three nautical miles — from Epidamnus, and then the always wind-obeying deep sea began to cause us alarm that we might be in danger. We did not long retain hope that we would be safe. The Heavens allowed us some obscured light to see by, and what we saw gave our fearful minds a dreadful certainty that we would immediately die.

"I myself would gladly have embraced death, but the incessant weeping of my wife, who mourned what she saw must come, and the piteous plaints of the pretty babes, who cried because that is what babies do — they were ignorant of the danger they were in and so did not know enough to be afraid — forced me to seek a way to delay their deaths and mine. This is what we did because we could find no wiser action to do.

"The sailors sought safety by taking the lifeboat and leaving the ship, which was about to sink, with us still aboard. My wife, more careful for the latter-born son — or was he the earlier-born son? — tied him to the end of a small spare mast such as seafaring men keep on board in case storms damage the mast. To our son one of the other twin sons — one of the two slaves — was tied. I myself tied the two remaining boys to the other side of the small spare mast.

"Having secured the children to the mast that would keep them afloat, my wife and I tied ourselves to the mast, one of us at each end. The ship sank, and we floated on the mast with the current, going straight, we thought, to Corinth.

"At length the Sun, gazing upon the Earth, dispersed the rain and fog that obscured our vision. The sea became calm, and we saw two ships from afar sailing straight to us from different directions. One ship I think came from Corinth; the other ship came from Epidaurus. Before they arrived — but let me stop speaking now. Guess what happened from what I have already told you."

"No, continue to speak, old man," the Duke of Ephesus said. "Do not stop speaking now. Perhaps we will pity — but not pardon — you."

Egeon said, "If the gods had pitied us, I would not now with good reason call them merciless to us! Before the two ships, which came from different directions, could travel ten leagues and meet, our floating mast hit a mighty rock with such force that the mast was split in two.

"In this unjust separation, my wife and I were both left with something to take delight in and something to take sorrow in. Her part of the mast was burdened with less weight than mine, but it was not burdened with less woe. The wind swept it away with more speed than it did my part of the mast, and I saw my wife and the two boys with her taken up into the ship carrying fishermen from Corinth, so we thought.

"Later, the other ship — the one from Epidaurus — rescued the other two boys and me. They knew who I was, and they gave an excellent welcome to their shipwrecked guests. They would have relieved the Corinthian fishermen of their catch — my wife and the two boys with her — but the ship from Epidaurus was very slow of sail, and therefore it sailed home to Epidaurus.

"Thus have you heard how I have been separated from happiness. My life of misfortunes has been prolonged, allowing me to tell the sad stories of my own life."

"For the sake of those whom you mourn," the Duke of Ephesus said, "do me the favor to tell in full what has befallen your family and you until now."

"My youngest boy — if indeed he is the youngest, for certainly he is the eldest boy in my care," Egeon said, "at eighteen years of age became curious about his brother. He begged me to allow him and his slave, whose brother had also been lost, to go out into the world and seek their lost brothers. Both of them had been given the names of their lost brothers as a way to honor those lost brothers. I allowed them to go. My sons were now both named Antipholus; the slaves were now both named Dromio. Out of love for and the hope of seeing the son who had been lost, I risked losing the son whom I had saved and raised. I allowed him to travel in search of his brother.

"A few years later, I decided to travel to find my lost son — or sons, as was now the case. I spent five summers traveling in furthest Greece and roaming through Asia and its furthest boundaries. Finally traveling homeward, I came to Ephesus. Here, I had no hope of finding my sons, yet I am loath to leave unsearched this town or any other town or any place where men may dwell.

"But here I must end the story of my life. I would be happy when I die if all my travels had assured me that my twin sons still live."

The Duke of Ephesus said, "Hapless Egeon, you are a man whom the Fates have marked to bear extreme and dire misfortune! Believe me, were it not against our laws, as well as against my crown, my oath, and my office — Princes may not go against these things, even if they would like to; instead, they must do their duty — my soul would argue in your favor.

"But, although you have been sentenced to die, and a sentence, once passed, may not be repealed without great damage to the Prince's honor, yet I will help you as much as I can. Therefore, merchant of Syracuse, I will allow you to spend this day raising money with which you can save your life. Go to all the friends you have here in Ephesus. Beg or borrow to raise the money and live. If you are unable to raise the money today, then you are doomed to die tonight. Jailer, keep him in your custody. Go with him as he attempts to raise money."

The jailer replied, "I will, my lord."

Egeon thought, *Hopeless and helpless does Egeon wend, but all he is doing is delaying his life's end.*

— 1.2 —

Three people arrived in the marketplace of Ephesus. They were Antipholus of Syracuse, Dromio of Syracuse, and a merchant who was a friend to Antipholus of Syracuse.

The merchant said to Antipholus of Syracuse, "For these reasons, you should say that you are from Epidamnus. If you do not, your possessions and money will be confiscated. This very day a merchant from Syracuse was arrested after he arrived here. Because he does not have enough money to pay the ransom for his life, he will die — as is the law of Ephesus — before the weary Sun sets in the West. Now I return to you your money that you gave to me for safekeeping."

Antipholus of Syracuse said to Dromio of Syracuse, "Take this money to the Centaur Inn, where we are staying, and stay there, Dromio, until I come to you. Within an hour, it will be time for the midday meal. Until then, I will view this town, look at the businesses and markets, gaze upon the buildings, and then return and sleep at the inn because I am stiff and weary from our long journey."

"You have asked me to take this money," Dromio of Syracuse said. "Many a man would take you at your word, and take the money and run, having so good an opportunity."

He took the money and exited.

Antipholus of Syracuse said to the merchant, "He is a trustworthy rascal, sir. Very often, when I am tired because of cares and melancholy, he brightens my mood by making merry jests. Will you walk with me about the town, and then go to my inn and dine with me?"

The merchant replied, "I am invited, sir, to visit certain merchants, in business with whom I hope to make considerable profit. Therefore, I beg your pardon, but I cannot eat dinner with you. However, if it is OK with you, at five o'clock, I will meet you at the marketplace and stay with you until bedtime. Because of my business, I must leave you now."

"Farewell until then," Antipholus of Syracuse said. "I will go and roam at random, wandering up and down to view the town."

"Sir, I leave you to your own devices, and I wish you happiness."

The merchant exited.

"He wishes me happiness," Antipholus of Syracuse said, "but happiness is the thing I cannot get. As I roam this world, I am like a drop of water that seeks another drop in the ocean. Falling into the ocean in an attempt to find his fellow, the drop of water — unseen by his fellow and inquisitive about his fellow — mingles with the other drops. Like that drop of water, I, unlucky as I attempt to find a mother and a brother, roam everywhere."

Dromio of Ephesus — not Dromio of Syracuse — now appeared on the scene.

Antipholus of Syracuse saw him and, mistaking him for Dromio of Syracuse, thought, *Here comes the almanac of my true birthdate. When I see him, I know how old I am because he and I were born on the same day.*

Antipholus of Syracuse said to Dromio of Ephesus, "What's happening? How is it that you have returned so soon?"

"Returned so soon!" Dromio of Ephesus said. "Rather, I have arrived too late. The capon — a castrated rooster — burns, and the pig is so over-cooked that it falls from the spit. The clock has struck twelve upon the bell — it is late for the midday meal! — and my mistress has struck me once upon my cheek. She is so hot because the meat is cold; the meat is cold because you have not come home; you have not come home because you have no appetite; and you have no stomach because you ate a big breakfast. But we who know what it is to fast and pray — to not eat while praying that you will return home soon so that all of your family can eat together — are paying the penalty for your absence from home today."

"Stop your windy breath, sir," Antipholus of Syracuse ordered. "Tell me this, please. Where have you left the money that I gave you?"

"Oh, the sixpence you gave me on Wednesday to pay the saddler for my mistress' crupper — the strap that goes around the horse's tail and keeps the saddle from sliding forward? I gave it to the saddler, sir. I did not keep it."

"I am not in the mood for jokes now," Antipholus of Syracuse replied. "Tell me, without jokes and without delay, where is the money?

We are strangers here, so how dare you allow so great a sum of money out of your sight?"

"Please, sir, joke when you are sitting down and eating dinner. I from my mistress have come to you posthaste. If I return without you, my head shall pay for it indeed. My mistress will treat me like a doorpost on which accounts are chalked up — that is, scored — in a tavern. The scores are marks, and my mistress will hit me and score a mark upon my head. Really, I think that your stomach, like mine, should be your clock, and should tell you when to strike out for home without the necessity of being sent a messenger."

"Come, Dromio, come, these jests are out of season; this is not the right time for such jokes. Reserve your jokes for a merrier hour than this. Where is the gold that I entrusted to you?"

"Entrusted to me, sir? Why, you gave no gold to me."

"Come on, Sir Rascal, stop your foolishness, and tell me what you have done with the money that I put you in charge of."

"My only charge has been to fetch you from the marketplace to the Phoenix, which is the name of your home, and a very good name it is, sir, to eat dinner. My mistress and her sister are waiting for you."

"Tell me in what safe place you have deposited my money," Antipholus of Syracuse said, "or I shall break that merry head of yours that keeps telling me jokes that I am not in the mood to hear. Where are the thousand marks that I gave to you?"

"I have some marks you made on my head," Dromio of Ephesus said, "and I have some marks my mistress made on my shoulders, but between the beatings I have received from the two of you I do not have a thousand marks. If I should return to your worship those particular marks, perhaps you would not bear them patiently."

"Your mistress' marks? What mistress — what female boss — do you have?"

"Your worship's wife, my mistress at the Phoenix, your home. She is hungry because she is fasting until you come home to dinner, and she really wishes that you would hurry home to dinner."

"What! Will you mock me to my face even after I have forbidden you to make jokes? There, take that, you rascal."

Antipholus of Syracuse took off his hat and started hitting Dromio of Ephesus with it. Both Antipholuses used their hats to hit their slaves. Both hats were made of a soft material and did not cause pain or leave a mark. Both Dromios screamed when they were hit with a hat because they loved to make noise and exaggerate and complain. The wife of Antipholus of Ephesus also caused no pain when she hit Dromio of Ephesus.

"What do you mean by this, sir?" Dromio shouted. "For God's sake, hold your hands and stop hitting me! If you will not, then I will take to my heels and run away!"

He ran away.

Antipholus of Syracuse said, "Upon my life, by some trick or other, this rascal has had all my money taken from him — by a cheat, no doubt. People say that this town of Ephesus is full of con men — nimble jugglers who deceive the eye, dark-working sorcerers who manipulate men's minds, soul-killing witches who deform the body, disguised cheaters, fast-talking mountebanks, and many similar engagers in sin. If that is true, it is a good reason to leave Ephesus all the sooner. I'll go to the Centaur Inn and look for Dromio. I greatly fear my money is not safe."

CHAPTER 2

In front of the house of Antipholus of Ephesus, his wife, who was named Adriana, and her sister, who was named Luciana, spoke together.

"Neither my husband nor the slave has returned," Adriana said. "I sent Dromio to quickly find his master. Surely, Luciana, it is two o'clock now."

"Perhaps some merchant invited your husband to eat with him, and from the marketplace he's gone somewhere to dinner on business. Good sister, let us dine and not worry about your husband. A man is master of his liberty as far as the women in his life are concerned; he comes and goes as he pleases. But when it comes to business, time is their master, and they come and go as their business demands of them. Chances are, your husband is attending to his business, so be patient, sister."

"Why should men have more liberty than women do?"

"Because their business always lies out of doors. They do not do their business at home."

Adriana said, "Look, whenever I act the way that he is acting now, he gets mad at me."

"He is your husband. He is the bridle of your will. A wife should obey her husband."

"Only asses should have such a bridle."

"Why, headstrong liberty is lashed with woe," Luciana said. "There's nothing under Heaven that men do not have dominion over, whether it is on land, in the sea, or in the sky. The female beasts, the female fishes, and the female winged fowls are their males' subjects; they are subjected to the males' control. Men, who are more divine than women because God created Adam before Eve and because God created Eve from the rib of Adam, are the masters of all these beasts, fish, and fowl. Men are the lords of the wide world and the wild watery seas. Men are endowed with intellectual sense and souls. Men have more preeminence than fish and fowls. Men are the masters and lords of their females. Therefore, you should obey your husband."

"This servitude of women to men is the reason you stay unwed," Adriana said.

"No, not this servitude," Luciana said. "Instead, I stay unwed because of the troubles of the marriage bed. I am not so much worried about obeying my husband, when I have one, as I am worried about my husband being unhappy and taking his unhappiness to bed. I am worried about him being unfaithful to me."

"But, if you were wedded, you would have some sway — some influence — over your husband."

"Before I learn to love a husband, I will learn how to obey a husband and make him happy."

"What would you do if your husband were to veer off the course of a stable marriage and start to pursue another woman?"

"I would endure it patiently until he returned to his true course and came home."

"If you could stay unmoved by your husband's infidelity, that would indeed be patience!" Adriana said. "It is no marvel that you are waiting to marry. Such meekness can be practiced while you have no cause not to be meek. A wretched soul, bruised with adversity, we tell to be quiet when we hear it cry. But were we burdened with a similar weight of pain, as much or more would we ourselves complain. Therefore, you — who have no unkind husband to make you grieve — would relieve my grief by urging me to be patient and enduring. But if you live to be married to an unkind husband, you will reject and leave behind you the foolish patience you advise me now to have."

"Well, I will marry one day and then I can put my ideas into practice," Luciana said.

She looked up and said, "Here comes your man Dromio now. Your husband must be near."

Adriana asked Dromio of Ephesus, "Is your tardy master now close at hand?"

"His two hands have been very close to me — my two ears are witness to that," he replied. "They have been boxed."

"Did you talk to him? Did he tell you what he intends to do? Do you know what is in his mind?" Adriana asked.

"He spoke his mind upon my ears," Dromio of Ephesus said. "Ask not for whom the hands told — they tolled blows upon my ears the way that the tongue of a bell tolls with blows. Damn his hands — I could scarcely hear the words he spoke and understand them."

Luciana asked, "Did he speak ambiguously, and so you could not understand his meaning?"

"No, he struck my ears so plainly that I could feel his blows very well. But he hit me so dreadfully that I could not understand what he was saying because I could not stand up under his blows."

"Please tell me," Adriana said, "whether he is coming home. It would seem that he would have a good reason for you to tell me if he is not coming home."

"He has a good reason indeed, mistress," Dromio said. "He is horn-mad."

"Horn-mad, you rascal!" Adriana said. "Are you saying that I have been unfaithful and cuckolded him and given him horns?"

"I do not mean that he is cuckold-mad. I mean that he is horn-mad in the sense of a horned beast such as a bull or stag that is so angry that it charges people and tries to hurt them with its horns. It is certain that he is stark raving mad. When I asked him to come home to dinner, he asked me for a thousand marks in gold. This conversation ensued:

"'It is dinnertime,' quoth I.

"'My gold!' quoth he.

"'Your meat does burn,' quoth I.

"'My gold!' quoth he.

"'Will you come home?' quoth I.

"'My gold!' quoth he. 'Where is the thousand marks I gave you, villain?'

"'The pig,' quoth I, 'is burned.'

"'My gold!' quoth he.

"'My mistress, sir,' quoth I.

"'To Hell with your mistress! I do not know your mistress; damn your mistress!'"

"Quoth whom?" Luciana asked.

"Quoth my master — your sister's husband," Dromio replied. 'I know,' quoth he, 'no house, no wife, no mistress.' I had thought that if he did not come home that he would give me a message to deliver to you with my tongue, but the only message I have brought home is the one that I carry on my shoulders — that is where he beat me."

"Go back to him, rascal, and bring him home," Adriana ordered.

"Go back again, and be beaten and sent home again? For God's sake, send some other messenger."

"Go back, slave, or I will hit you across your head," Adriana said.

"And he will bless that cross by giving me another beating across my head. Between you I shall have a holy head. In fact, if you two hit me hard enough, my head will be full of holes."

"Go now, prating peasant!" Adriana said. "Fetch your master home." She made a motion as if she were going to kick Dromio.

"Am I so round with you as you are with me, that like you would a soccer ball you must spurn me with your foot? You spurn me hence, and he will spurn me hither. If I am to last in this service, you must encase me in leather for my protection."

Dromio exited.

Luciana said, "Your impatience really shows in your face right now."

"My husband favors his female tramps with his presence," Adriana said, "while I stay at home and starve for lack of his merry looks and company.

"Has increasing age taken my former alluring beauty from my poor cheeks and replaced it with homeliness? If so, then my husband has wasted my beauty by ignoring me. Are my discourses dull? Is my wit barren? Am I unable to say interesting things? If my former voluble and sharp discourse is marred, it is my husband's unkindness that blunts it more than ever hard marble could. Do his female tramps entice him with their gay and pretty clothing? It is his fault that I do not have better clothing to wear — he controls my household expenses.

"The faults that are found in me are faults that he caused. He is the reason for my ruin. He could easily and quickly restore my decayed beauty with a sunny look, but he is an unruly dear — like a deer that breaks out of its enclosure, he breaks out of the walls of his home and eats away from home.

"Poor me! He does not treat me like he should treat his wife — he treats me as if I were a laughingstock! I can imagine his female tramps and him laughing at me!"

"This is self-harming jealousy," Luciana said. "Get rid of it."

"Unfeeling fools can easily get rid of such jealousy," Adriana said. "They do not feel the pain that I feel. I know my husband's eyes feast on other women outside our home; otherwise, he would be here right now. Sister, you know that my husband promised to give me a necklace. I would gladly give up the necklace if my husband would be faithful to me!

"An enameled piece of jewelry can lose its beauty, yet the gold in it will remain valuable. This is true of aging husbands and wives. Unfortunately, others can touch the gold, and if the gold is often touched, the gold can wear away, thus making the jewelry less valuable. Similarly, a man can be touched if he gives in to temptation, thus making the man less valuable. No man who has a good reputation should shame it with falsehoods and corruption. I believe that my husband is golden, but he is allowing his female tramps to wear away his gold. Because my beauty can no longer please my husband's eyes, I'll weep what's left of my beauty away, and die as I weep."

How many fond fools serve mad jealousy! Luciana thought. *Adriana is fond of her husband, and she suffers from excessive jealousy.*

— 2.2 —

Standing in a public place, Antipholus of Syracuse said, "The gold I gave to Dromio has been safely deposited at the Centaur Inn and the heedful, competent slave has wandered forth to seek me. By my own calculation and the information I received from the inn's host, I do not see how it is possible for me to have so recently seen Dromio — there simply has not been enough time. This is puzzling, but it did happen. I see Dromio coming toward me now."

Dromio of Syracuse walked up to him.

"How are you now, sir?" Antipholus of Syracuse said. "Is your merry mood altered? If you love beatings, jest with me again. You never heard of the Centaur Inn? You never received gold from me? Your female boss sent you to bring me home to dinner? My home is named the Phoenix? Were you insane when you said such things to me?"

"What?" Dromio of Syracuse said. "When did I ever say such things?"

"You said these things to me just now, right here, not half an hour ago."

"I have not seen you since you sent me from here to go to the Centaur Inn with the gold you gave me."

"Rascal, you denied ever having received gold from me, and you told me that you had a female boss and that she had a dinner waiting for me. I hope that your head, which I beat, felt that I was displeased."

"I am glad to see you in this merry mood," Dromio of Syracuse said, "but what do you mean by this jest? Please, master, tell me."

"Do you think I am joking? Do you mock me to my face? Here, take this, and take that!"

Antipholus of Syracuse took off his hat and struck Dromio of Syracuse twice.

"Stop, sir, for God's sake! Now your joke has turned serious. Why are you beating me? This is not part of any bargain that I made."

"Why am I beating you? Sometimes I am in a good mood and I let you be my jester and make jokes and engage in fun conversation. But you are so saucy that you go too far and make jokes when I am in a serious mood. You even treat my hours for serious work as if they were happy hours at a public tavern.

"Remember this proverb: When the Sun shines, let foolish gnats make sport, but let them creep in crannies when the Sun hides its beams. In other words, there is a right time for all things. There is a right time for jokes, and there is a right time for serious business. If you want to jest with me, look at my face and determine my mood. Once you know my mood, you can fashion your behavior so that it is appropriate for my mood. If you do not take my advice, I will beat my advice into your sconce."

"Sconce?" Dromio of Syracuse said. "You are using the word 'sconce'? Showing off your vocabulary, are you? Although I am only a slave, I know that sconce has three meanings. One, it can mean a head. Two, it can mean a small fort. Three, it can mean a protective screen. If you should stop beating me as if you were using a battering ram against a fortress, I would prefer 'sconce' to mean a head. But if you continue to beat me, I must get a sconce — a small fort — to protect my head and ensconce my head with a protective screen for further protection. Otherwise, you will beat my head into my shoulders. But, sir, why are you beating me?"

"Don't you know?"

"All I know, sir, is that you are beating me."

"Shall I tell you why I am beating you?" Antipholus of Syracuse asked.

"Yes, sir, and tell me wherefore, for they say every why has a wherefore."

"Let me explain the 'why' first. I am beating you because you mocked me. Now let me explain the 'wherefore.' I am beating you because you mocked me a second time."

"Was there ever any man thus beaten out of season, when the 'why' and the 'wherefore' have neither rhyme nor reason? I don't think that any man has ever been beaten for less reason than I have been today. Well, sir, I thank you."

"Thank me for what?" Antipholus of Syracuse asked.

"I thank you because you gave me something for nothing."

"I will make that up to you by giving you nothing for something, but isn't it time for the midday meal?"

"No, sir," Dromio of Syracuse said. "It can't be time for dinner. If it were time, the meat would be ready, but it lacks something that I have."

"What is that?" Antipholus of Syracuse asked.

"Tenderizing."

"The best way to tenderize a steak is to beat it with a meat mallet. If the meat has not been tenderized, then it will be tough."

"If it is tough, sir, I beg you not to eat it."

"What is your reason?" Antipholus of Syracuse asked.

"If you try to eat tough steak, it might make you angry, and then you would tenderize me."

"Dromio, learn the right time to make a joke. There's a right time for all things."

"I would have dared to deny that that is true — before you became so angry at me."

"By what rule of logic and argumentation would you deny that?" Antipholus of Syracuse asked.

"I would deny it, master, by a rule as plain as the plain bald pate of Father Time himself."

"Let's hear your reasoning."

"There is no right time that a man who grows bald naturally — from old age — can recover his hair. Therefore, there is not a time for everything."

"Couldn't he recover his hair by fine and recovery? That is a way for men to get legal possession of property."

"Yes, master, a man can pay a fine fee for a wig and thus recover the lost hair of another man. The best wigs are made from real hair."

"Why is Time such a niggard of hair, being, as hair is, so plentiful an outgrowth?" Antipholus of Syracuse asked.

"Hair is a blessing that Father Time bestows on furry beasts; what Father Time has scanted men in hair he has given them in intelligence."

"Objection! Many men have more hair than intelligence."

"Men who have more hair than intelligence still have enough intelligence to lose their hair. They pursue the wrong kind of women, catch syphilis, and lose their hair as a consequence of the disease."

"Didn't you just now conclude that hairy men are straightforward, candid plain dealers who lack the intelligence needed to be deceptive and engage in fraudulent behavior?" Antipholus of Syracuse asked.

"Plain dealers take what is called the direct approach with women, sir. Their idea of flirting is to say 'Fancy a f**k?' The plainer the dealer, the quicker he is to catch syphilis and lose his hair. At least he has a policy in mind when he grows bald."

"What is the reason for the policy?" Antipholus of Syracuse asked.

"There are two reasons, sir, and they are sound reasons."

"Sound?" Antipholus of Syracuse said. "I doubt it."

"Sure reasons, then."

"Nope. I am still doubtful. I suspect a falsehood."

"Certain ones then."

"Name them, and let's see if they are certain," Antipholus of Syracuse said.

"The first reason is the money he will save in haircuts, and the second reason is that no longer will a hair fall into his soup."

"All this time you have tried to prove that not everything has a right time," Antipholus of Syracuse said.

"Yes, and I did prove that, sir. There is no right time — or any time at all — that a man who grows bald naturally can recover his hair."

"But your reasoning was not substantial; why, the reasoning is so off that your debating opponents have no time to recover from your arguments because your opponents are stunned by your arguments' silliness."

"Therefore, I will improve my argument: Time himself is bald and therefore until the world ends Time will have bald followers. Anyone who follows Father Time will grow old and will grow bald."

"I knew you would have a bald conclusion," Antipholus of Syracuse said.

He looked up and said, "Look! Two women — I don't know who they are — are beckoning for us to go over to them."

A wondering look on his face, Antipholus of Syracuse, accompanied by Dromio of Syracuse, walked over to the two women, who were Adriana and Luciana.

"Yes, Antipholus, look at me as if I were a stranger and frown at me," Arianna said. "Some other woman has your looks of love. Pretend that I am not Adriana and pretend that I am not your wife. At one time, without being urged, you would spend time with me. You would tell me that words were never music to your ear unless I had spoken them. You would tell me that an object was never pleasing to your eye unless I had shown it to you. You would tell me that a touch was never welcome to your hand unless I was holding hands with you. You would tell me that meat was never tasty unless I had carved the meat for you.

"How did it come to be, husband, that you are now estranged from yourself? You and I are married, and in marriage two become one. You and I are one undividable whole, incorporate. By being joined with you, I am better than I would be by myself alone. How then can you regard me as a stranger? I am part of you, and the two of us make up you. Do not try to tear yourself away from me! Know, my love, you can separate the two of us as easily as you can put a drop of water into the churning sea and take out that exact drop of water, with nothing added to it or taken away from it. If you try to take me out of yourself, you will find the task impossible because we are one being, not two.

"It would hurt me deeply and touch me to the quick if you were ever to hear that I were licentious and that this body, which is consecrated to you, had been contaminated by ruffian lust! If that should ever happen, wouldn't you spit at me and kick me and scream at me that I am married to you? The forehead reveals character — wouldn't you tear the stained skin from my harlot's brow and tear my wedding ring from my finger and break my wedding ring with a deep vow of divorce?

"I know that you are capable of doing those things, and therefore I believe that you would do those things. You should know that in fact I have been stained by adultery; my blood has been mingled with the sin of lust. What do I mean by this? You and I are one, and if you commit adultery, then I am contaminated by the adultery you committed — the poison of your adultery infects my blood, and that contamination makes me a whore. Therefore, if you keep your marriage vows and sleep in the bed of the wife you married, I will live unstained and you will live without dishonor."

"Why are you saying these things to me, pretty woman?" Antipholus of Syracuse asked. "I do not know you. I have been in Ephesus for only two hours. This town and your conversation are both strange to me. I have heard every word you said to me, but I do not understand even one word of what you have said."

Luciana said, "For shame, brother-in-law! You have changed! When have you ever treated my sister like this! She sent Dromio to you to bring you home for dinner."

"She sent Dromio to me?"

Dromio of Syracuse said, "She sent me?"

Adriana said, "Yes, I sent you, Dromio. And when you returned from seeing him, you said that he had beaten you, and as he was beating you, he said that he did not live in this house and he said that I was not his wife."

Antipholus of Syracuse asked Dromio of Syracuse, "Did you talk, sir, with this gentlewoman? Are you confederates with her? What plot did you two form?"

"I talk to her, sir?" Dromio of Syracuse replied. "I have never even seen her until now!"

"Rascal, you are lying," Antipholus of Syracuse said. "I know that you are lying because you earlier said to me in the marketplace exactly the things that she said she told you to say to me."

"I have never spoken to her in my entire life."

"How then is it possible that she knows our names and calls us by them? Is she perhaps clairvoyant?"

Adriana said to Antipholus of Syracuse, "You are supposed to be a serious man, yet you conspire disgustingly with your slave to deceive me and make me angry! Perhaps I must suffer because of your estrangement from me, but do not make that wrong worse by treating me with contempt.

"I will hold on to your sleeve. You, my husband, are a strong elm tree. I, your wife, am a weak vine. Although I am weak, I am married to your strength, and therefore I share your strength. If anything possesses you except me, it is dross; it is usurping, parasitic ivy, a brier, or worthless moss that, because it has not been cut off, infects your sap and lives by harming you."

Antipholus of Syracuse thought, *She is talking to me. She is talking about me. Was I married to her in a dream? Am I dreaming now and thinking that I am hearing all of this? What error is making our — her and my — eyes and ears behave this way? Until I know for sure what is happening, I will pretend that this delusion is reality.*

Luciana ordered, "Dromio, go and tell the servants to set the table for dinner."

Dromio of Syracuse said, "I wish I had my rosary beads! At least I — sinner that I am — can cross myself. This is the fairyland! Oh, spite of spites! We are talking with goblins, changelings, and sprites. Unless we obey them, this will ensue: Witches in the form of owls will suck away our breath, or fairies will pinch us black and blue."

Luciana said, "Why are you talking to yourself and not answering me? Dromio, the Greek word *dromeos* means runner, but you are a drone, a snail, a slug, a foolish blockhead!"

"I have been transformed, master, haven't I?" Dromio of Syracuse asked.

"I think that your mind has been transformed in some way, and so has mine."

"Master, I think that I have been transformed both in mind and in body."

"You still have your own body."

"No, I am sure that I have not. I am an ape. I am a counterfeit — or perhaps I am a fool. Or I am both."

Luciana said, "If you have been changed into anything, then you have been changed into an ass."

"That is true," Dromio of Syracuse said. "She rides me — she teases and criticizes me. And I long for grass — I long to go to pasture and be relieved of responsibility and have freedom. If I were not an ass, then I would know her as well as she knows me."

Adriana said, "Let us stop this foolishness. I decline to act like a foolish child and weep while my husband and his slave laugh at all my sorrows."

She said to Antipholus of Syracuse, "Come, sir, let us go in our house and eat."

She said, "Dromio, keep the door."

She added, "Husband, I'll dine upstairs with you today and listen to your confession of a thousand idle pranks."

She said to Dromio of Syracuse, "If anyone asks you for your master, say that he is dining away from home and let no one enter the house. We do not want to be disturbed."

She said to Luciana, "Come, sister."

She finished by saying, "Dromio, do your job as doorkeeper well."

Antipholus of Syracuse thought, *Am I on Earth, in Heaven, or in Hell? Am I sleeping or waking? Am I insane or in my right mind? Do these people know me and I don't know myself? I'll say as they say and do as they do and continue in this course of action despite all the confusion. I will continue in this course of action no matter what are the risks and consequences.*

Dromio of Syracuse asked him, "Master, shall I be the porter at the door? Shall I be the doorkeeper?"

Adriana answered for him, "Yes, and let no one enter, lest I break your pate — your head."

Luciana said, "Come, come, Antipholus, we dine too late."

They left to eat dinner.

CHAPTER 3

Before the house of Antipholus of Ephesus were standing Antipholus of Ephesus; Dromio of Ephesus; Angelo, who was a goldsmith of Ephesus; and Balthazar, who was a merchant of Ephesus.

"Good Signior Angelo, please excuse us," Antipholus of Ephesus said. "My wife is shrewish when I come home late. Please say that I lingered with you at your shop so that I could see you make her necklace. Also, please say that you will bring it here tomorrow. But look here at my slave. He is a rascal who would impudently swear that he met me in the marketplace and that I beat him, and that I said I had given him a thousand marks in gold, and that I denied that I was married to my wife and lived in my house."

He said to Dromio of Ephesus, "You drunkard, what did you mean by saying all of this?"

"Say what you will, sir, but I know what I know. I know that you beat me in the marketplace. I can prove it with evidence from your own hand. If my skin were made of parchment, and the blows you gave me were ink, your own handwriting on my back and shoulders would tell you what I think."

"I know what I think: I think you are an ass," Antipholus of Ephesus said.

"Indeed, judging from the wrongs I suffer and the blows I bear, it does appear that I am an ass. I should kick back when I am kicked. If I would do that when I am in such a predicament, you would keep away from my heels and beware of this ass."

Antipholus of Ephesus said, "You're solemn, Signior Balthazar. I pray to God that our entertainment and meal will show you my good will toward you and that you are welcome here."

"Your welcome and friendship are much more valuable to me than your most excellent delicacies," Balthazar replied.

"Signior Balthazar, whether one is served flesh or fish, a hearty welcome is not a substitute for a good meal. A hearty welcome cannot make up for a bad meal. As we know, a hearty welcome is not the equal of even one good course."

"Good food, sir, is common," Balthazar said. "Every man can provide that."

"And a good welcome is even more common than good food," Antipholus of Ephesus said. "All that is required for a good welcome is words."

"A little food and a great big welcome makes a merry feast," Balthazar said.

"Yes, to a niggardly host, and to a guest who eats less than the host, but though my food is mean, eat it with my best wishes for you," Antipholus of Ephesus said. "You may eat better food elsewhere, but it will not be served to you with a better heart than mine."

He tried to open the door of his house, but it would not budge. He said, "That's odd. My door is locked. Dromio, call for someone to unlock the door and let us in."

Dromio called, "Maud, Bridget, Marian, Cicel, Gillian, Ginn!"

Antipholus of Ephesus was a successful man with many servants.

Dromio of Syracuse, who was serving as porter, called from inside the house, "Blockhead, drudge, cuckold, fool, idiot, clown! Either go away, or shut up! Are you trying to use a spell to get women by calling the names of so many? One woman is one too many. Go, get away from the door."

Dromio of Ephesus said, "Which fool has been made our porter? My master is out here waiting in the street."

Dromio of Syracuse said, "Let him walk from here to wherever he came from — that will keep his feet from growing cold."

Antipholus of Ephesus said, "Who is talking from inside my house? Whoever you are, open the door!"

"Right, sir," Dromio of Syracuse replied. "I will tell you when I will open the door after you tell me a good reason why I should open the door."

"Why should you open the door? You should open the door so that I can eat my dinner. I have not eaten today."

"You will not eat here today," Dromio of Syracuse replied. "Come again — when you are invited."

"Who are you who is keeping me out of my own house — the house I own?"

"Right now, I have the job of the porter, sir, and my name is Dromio."

"Rascal!" Dromio of Ephesus exclaimed. "You have stolen both my job and my name. The one never got me credit; the other always got me much blame. If you had been Dromio today in my place in the marketplace, you would have changed your job as porter for that of a target for blows and you would have changed your name of Dromio to the name of Ass. To have avoided that fate, you would have to have changed your face from that of mine or have changed your name from Dromio to another human name to avoid being beaten like an ass."

Antipholus of Syracuse started to bang on the door.

Luce, a servant to Adriana, now arrived and said, "What a turmoil I hear! Dromio, who are these people banging on the door?"

Dromio of Ephesus recognized Luce's voice and said, "Let my master in, Luce."

Luce replied, "No, your master comes too late. Tell your master that."

She knew that the meal had already been served and was being eaten. She also thought that her master was upstairs eating, not growing angry outside the door.

"I have to laugh at that," Dromio of Ephesus said. "Let me have at you with some words: Shall I come in with my staff? Shall I make myself at home?"

"Let me have at you with some other words," Luce replied. "When should you come in? Can you tell? The answer is never. If you come in here, you will need more than just a staff — you will need an entire army."

From inside the house, Dromio of Syracuse said, "Luce — if your name is Luce — you have answered him well."

Antipholus of Ephesus yelled, "Can you hear, minion? Let us in! Please?"

Luce replied, "I have already answered your question with my own questions: 'When should you come in? Can you tell?'"

Dromio of Syracuse said to Luce, "You have already answered the question: 'The answer is never.'"

Antipholus of Ephesus pounded on the door.

Dromio of Ephesus said, "Well struck! You answered a verbal blow from Luce with a physical blow on the door."

Antipholus of Ephesus yelled, "Luce, you baggage, you good-for-nothing woman, let me in."

"Let you in? Says who?" Luce yelled.

"Master, knock hard on the door," Dromio of Ephesus said.

"Let him knock until the door aches," Luce yelled.

Antipholus of Ephesus yelled, "You'll regret this, minion, if I beat the door down."

Luce replied, "Not likely, since we have a pair of stocks in this town. The police will put you in the stocks, and *I* will torment *you*."

Hearing all the racket, Adriana arrived and said, "Who is it at the door who keeps making all this noise?"

From inside the house, Dromio of Syracuse replied, "Truly, your town is troubled with unruly fellows."

"Is that you, wife?" Antipholus said. "I wish that you had arrived earlier."

Adriana, thinking that her husband was upstairs eating dinner, said, "Your wife, Sir Rascal! Go and get away from the door! Get out of here!"

Dromio of Ephesus said, "If Sir Rascal is sent away in pain, then I — a regular rascal — will indeed suffer sorely."

"Here is neither a meal, sir, nor a welcome," Angelo said. "We would be happy to have either."

Balthazar said, "We have been debating whether good food or a good welcome is better, but it looks like we shall depart with neither."

"Your guests are standing at the door, master," Dromio of Ephesus said cheekily. "Tell them that they are welcome in your home."

"There is something in the wind — some reason why we cannot get in," Antipholus of Ephesus said. "Something is wrong."

"Something in the wind?" Dromio of Ephesus said. "That would be us. You would know that a cold wind is blowing if your clothing were made of thinner material. Your food inside the house is warm, but you are standing out here in the cold. It makes a man as angry as a mad-horn horned buck to be so treated."

Antipholus of Ephesus ordered, "Go and fetch me some tool that I can use to break down the door."

Dromio of Syracuse said, "Break anything here, and I'll break your rascally head."

Dromio of Ephesus said, "A man may break a word with you, sir, and words are but wind, and therefore I will break wind in your face and not in a direction away from you."

Dromio of Syracuse said, "It seems that you want your head broken. Damn you, rascal!"

Dromio of Ephesus said, "I am spending way too much time in the great out of doors — let me in! Please!"

Dromio of Syracuse replied, "Yes, I will let you in — when fowls have no feathers and fish have no fins."

Antipholus of Ephesus said to Dromio of Ephesus, "Well, I'll break in. Go and borrow a crowbar."

Dromio of Ephesus willfully misunderstood what his master had said: "A crow bare? A crow without feathers? Master, do you mean it? For every fish without a fin, there's a fowl without a feather. If a crow bare will get us inside the house, we will pluck a crow together. Once we are inside the house, then that Dromio and this Dromio can settle our argument."

Antipholus of Ephesus said, "Stop fooling around! Go! Bring back an iron crowbar."

"Be patient, sir," Balthazar said. "Don't break down your own door. If you do, you will harm your reputation and you will make people suspect that your wife has disobeyed you and dishonored you. So far, her reputation as a wife has been excellent. Consider this: You have long known that your wife is wise, that she is sober and virtuous, and that she is mature and modest. Because of this, you should conclude that she has a good reason — unknown to you right now — for locking the door and keeping you out of your own house. This reason she will explain to you later.

"Take my advice. Depart quietly now, and let all of us go and eat dinner at the Tiger Inn. Around evening, return — alone — to your house and talk to your wife about why she locked the door against you. If you use your strong hands to break down the door now, you will cause rumors to be spread by crowds of people. So far, your reputation is unblemished. Keep it that way, or people will remember the day you broke your own door down — and they will remember it even when you die. Gossip spreads from person to person to person, and everyone who hears the gossip remembers it."

"You are right," Antipholus of Ephesus said. "I will leave quietly. Although I am in no mood to be merry, and my wife obviously does not want me to be merry, I will change my mood — with effort — and stop being angry and instead be merry. I know a courtesan who converses well and excellently. She is pretty and witty; she is wild and yet she is gentle. We will dine with her.

"My wife has often accused me — unjustly — of having an affair with this woman whom I am talking about, but I swear that I am faithful to my wife and that I have never slept with this woman although I like looking at and talking to her. I would tell you if I had slept with her — we are all guys here, and the story would be a good one to tell in the locker room if I were the kind of man who has affairs. We will go to her house for dinner."

He said to Angelo, "Go to your home and fetch the necklace — it should be finished by this time. Bring it to the Porcupine, which is the name of the courtesan's home. If for no other reason than to spite my wife, I will give the necklace to the courtesan. Good sir, make haste. Since my own door refuses to open up for me, I'll knock elsewhere and see if that door will disdain me."

"I'll meet you at the Porcupine an hour or so from now," Angelo said.

"Please do," Antipholus of Ephesus said. "This jest at my wife's expense shall also cost me some expense."

— 3.2 —

Luciana and Antipholus of Syracuse had finished dining with her sister, Adriana, and now they were talking together.

Luciana said to Antipholus of Syracuse, whom she thought was married to her sister, "Is it possible that you have forgotten the duty of a husband? Antipholus, this is still the spring of your love for Adriana. Have the roots of your love for her started to rot so early? Shall a love that should vigorously grow instead lie in ruins? If you wed my sister only because of her wealth, then for the sake of her wealth treat her with more kindness.

"If you like another woman, then like that woman stealthily and not openly. Conceal your false love by acting in such a way that my sister is blind to it. Do not let my sister look at you and know by looking at you that you like another woman. Make sure that your tongue does not speak of the other woman. Look sweetly at my sister, treat my sister well, and mask your infidelity by appearing to be faithful. Although you engage in vice, appear to be the friend of virtue. Look as if you are a good husband, even though another woman has tainted your heart. Teach sin to appear like a holy saint. Be unfaithful to my sister in secret — she need not know. Why should a thief brag about his crimes? It is a double sin to be unfaithful in bed and to let your wife know during dinner that you are unfaithful. A sinful, shameful man can have a good reputation if he acts discreetly, but a bad deed becomes doubly bad when done indiscreetly.

"We poor women! We are trusting. We easily believe that you love us. You may like another woman in your heart, but as long as outward appearances make it seem that you love us, you can control us as you wish and we will orbit you the way that a planet orbits the Sun. Therefore, gentle brother-in-law, go inside the house again. Comfort my sister, cheer her up, and call her your wife. Tell some white lies and flatter her — the sweet breath of flattery conquers strife."

"Sweet mistress," Antipholus of Syracuse said, "I do not know your name, and I do not know by what miracle you know my name. Your knowledge and your grace are the equal of the wonders of the divine Earth.

"Teach me, dear creature, how to think and speak. My understanding is Earth-bound and smothered in errors; it is feeble, shallow, and weak. Reveal to me the hidden meaning of your words, which accuse me of deceit. My soul is pure and guiltless, and yet you are accusing me of marital infidelity — something that I have never been guilty of; after all, I am not married. Are you a goddess? Are you trying to make me into something that I am not? Transform me then, and to your power I'll yield. I am willing to change in order to please you.

"But if I am who I think I am, then I know well that your weeping sister is not my wife. I am not married to her, and I owe no allegiance to her wedding bed. I am inclined to love you far, far more than I am to love her.

"Sweet mermaid — sweet Siren — do not sing a song that will drown me in your sister's flood of tears. Sing a song that will encourage me to love you, and I will madly dote on you. Spread your golden hairs over the silver waves, and maiden, I will lie on your hair as if it were a bed. In that glorious daydream, I would think that death would be a benefit if I could die — while having an orgasm — in your lap. True love is light and therefore floats. You inspire love in me, and true love is the kind of love I hope that you inspire.

"But if you are a Siren urging me on to my destruction here in Ephesus, this town of magic, then the love you inspire in me is false and I hope that the false love will sink and drown."

Luciana said, "Are you insane? You must be, if you can think such thoughts!"

"I am not mad, but I am amazed and I hope to be mated — with you, the woman whom I love. How all of these things are occurring here in Ephesus, I do not know."

"You have a fault that your eyes have caused," Luciana said, thinking, *He has fallen in love with me because he thinks that I am beautiful. This is lust, not true love. He is married to my sister!*

"My eyes have been blinded by the sunny beams of your beauty," Antipholus of Syracuse said.

"Gaze at the beauty of the woman you should gaze at, and all will be well. Gaze at my sister."

"It is as good to close one's eyes, sweet love, as to look on night."

"Do not call me your love. Call my sister your love."

"I will call your sister's sister my love."

"My family has three daughters, one of whom lives far away. My sister's sister is my sister."

"Your sister's sister is you, and you are the better part of my own self. You are my eye's clearer eye and my dear heart's dearer heart. You are my food, my fortune, and the goal of my sweet hope. You are my only Heaven on Earth, and you make me believe in Heaven hereafter."

"All this is what my sister is to you — or should be."

"Call yourself your sister, sweetheart, because I am one with you. I will love you and I will spend my life with you. You have no husband, and I have no wife. Give me your hand."

"Wait! Stay here. I will go and get my sister. I want to know what she thinks of all this, and I want her to know that I am behaving properly. I value her opinion of me."

As Luciana exited, Dromio of Syracuse ran up to Antipholus of Syracuse, who asked, "How are you, Dromio? Why are you running so fast?"

"Do you know me, sir? Am I Dromio? Am I your slave? Am I myself?"

"You are Dromio, you are my slave, you are yourself."

"I am an ass, I am a woman's man, and I am besides myself."

"Which woman's man are you, and how are you besides yourself?" Antipholus of Syracuse asked.

"I am besides myself because I am owed to a woman — one who claims me, one who haunts me, one who will have me."

"What claim does she have on you?" Antipholus of Syracuse asked.

"The claim she has on me is like the claim you would have on a horse — she says that she owns me. This is beastly. I do not mean that I am a beast, but I do mean that that beastly woman is laying claim to me."

"Who is she?" Antipholus of Syracuse asked.

"She is a very reverent body — no one can talk about her without apologizing to God for the foul language necessary to describe her. I have only lean luck in this wedding match, and yet she makes her part of it a wondrously fat marriage."

"What do you mean by a fat marriage?" Antipholus of Syracuse asked.

"Sir, she is the kitchen wench and she is all grease; I don't know what to do with her except to make a lamp of her and run away from her by the light she will make. I bet that the rags she wears and the tallow in them will burn for the length of a harsh winter in Poland. If she lives until doomsday, she will burn a week longer than the whole world."

"What complexion does she have?" Antipholus of Syracuse asked.

"Swarthy, like my shoe, but her face is not kept half as clean. She sweats so much that you would be up to your ankles in perspiration."

"That's a fault that soap and water will mend."

"No, sir. Her dirt is too engrained. Noah's flood could not clean her face."

"What's her name?" Antipholus of Syracuse asked.

"Nell. 'Ell' with an 'n' in front. Her name is fitting because she is more than an ell. Her name and three quarters — that's an ell and three quarters of an ell — will not measure her from hip to hip. Remember, please, that an ell is forty-five inches."

"So she bears some breadth?" Antipholus of Syracuse asked.

"She is no longer from head to foot than from hip to hip; she is spherical, like a globe; I could find out the locations of countries by looking at her."

"In what part of her body stands Ireland?" Antipholus of Syracuse asked.

"In her buttocks. I found Ireland's bogs by looking at Nell's spongy, boggy backside."

"Where is Scotland?" Antipholus of Syracuse asked.

"A ness is a promontory or cape, and Scotland has many place names with that word including the Loch Ness. We non-Scots think of Scotland as being a barren place, and I found Scotland in the barrenness of the hard calluses in the palm of her hand."

"Where is France?" Antipholus of Syracuse asked.

"In her forehead; France is armed and in revolt, making war against her hair. She has a receding hairline and will soon be bald."

"Where is England?" Antipholus of Syracuse asked.

"I looked for the chalky white cliffs of Dover in her mouth, but I could find no whiteness in her teeth, so I guess that rainy England is located in her chin, because of all the perspiration that rains down her face from France."

"Where is Spain?" Antipholus of Syracuse asked.

"I did not see hot Spain, but I felt it in the hot breath coming from her nostrils."

"Where are America and the Indies?" Antipholus of Syracuse asked.

"Where are those fabulously wealthy areas of land? I saw them in her nose, which was decorated with rubies, valuable bright red carbuncles, and sapphires, which are also known as pimples, bright red lumpy boils, and pustules. Spain does a flourishing trade with America and the Indies, sending ships to take on cargo, and perspiration drips down Nell's nose and gets in her Spanish nostrils."

"Where are the Low Countries, including Belgium and the Netherlands?" Antipholus of Syracuse asked.

"Oh, sir, I did not look so low and so I did not see her nether regions.

"To conclude, this drudge, or witch, laid claim to me, called me Dromio, swore I was engaged to marry her, and told me what private marks I had on my body, including the birthmark on my shoulder, the mole on my neck, and the big wart on my left arm. Shocked and amazed by such knowledge, I ran from her as if she were a witch. I believe that if my breast had not been made of faith — I am protected by the metaphorical breastplate of righteousness and by my heart of steel — she would have transformed me into a dog with a docked tail and made me tread a wheel that would turn a spit in the kitchen."

Antipholus of Syracuse said, "Go and hurry down to the port. If the wind blows in any direction away from shore, we will not stay in this town tonight. If any ship is going to set sail, come to the marketplace. I will wait there until you return to me. Everyone knows us here in Ephesus, although we know no one. That isn't right. This must be a town full of witches and magicians, and it is time, I think, for us to leave, to go, and to depart."

"As from a bear a man would run for his life," Dromio said, "so will I fly from her who would be my wife."

He exited.

Antipholus of Syracuse said to himself, "No one but warlocks and witches live here, and therefore it is high time that I not be here. A woman here calls me her husband, but I abhor her as a wife. She has a beautiful sister, who has such gentle graciousness and such enchanting presence and such marvelous conversation. But if everyone here is a witch, then she is a witch, too, although she seems to be a goddess. She has almost made me a traitor to myself, assuming that she is trying to tempt me to my doom, like a mermaid who is a Siren who sings beautifully so that sailors jump from their safe ships and swim to her dangerous shore. To prevent myself from succumbing to her temptation, I will figuratively, like Ulysses did literally, put wax in my ears so that I cannot hear her Siren song."

Angelo, carrying a necklace, walked up to Antipholus of Syracuse and said, "Master Antipholus —"

"Yes, that's my name."

"I know it is, sir. Look, here is the necklace. I hoped to have taken it to you at the Porcupine, but I needed to stay in my goldsmith shop and finish it."

"What do you want me to do with this?" Antipholus of Syracuse asked.

"Whatever you want, sir. I made it for you."

"Made it for me, sir!" Antipholus of Syracuse said. "I did not order it to be made."

"Yes, you did — not once, nor twice, but twenty times. Go home with it and make your wife happy. Soon, at suppertime, I'll visit you and you can pay me for the necklace."

Angelo thought, *I delayed coming to the Porcupine with the necklace on purpose. My respected and respectable friend should give the necklace to his wife and not to a courtesan. Also, the necklace should help resolve whatever quarrel my friend and his wife are having.*

"Please, sir, take the money now, for fear you will never again see the necklace or the money," Antipholus of Syracuse said.

"Funny! You are a merry man, sir. I will see you later."

Angelo exited.

Antipholus of Syracuse said to himself, "What I should think of this, I cannot tell. But I think that no man is so silly that he would refuse so beautiful a necklace when it is offered to him. I see that a man need not be a con man to live here — not when people in the streets simply hand over to him such golden gifts. I will go to the marketplace and wait for Dromio. If any ship is leaving this town, then we will board it."

CHAPTER 4

— 4.1 —

In a public place stood three people: the goldsmith Angelo, a merchant to whom he owed money, and a police officer who was dressed in the tough leather uniform that the police officers of Ephesus customarily wore for protection.

The merchant said to Angelo, "You know that the money you owe me was due at Pentecost, which is always fifty days after Easter, counting Easter as one of the days. I have not much bothered you by asking for the money you owe to me, and I would not do so now, but I must travel to Persia, and therefore I need money for my voyage. Therefore, pay me immediately, or I will be forced to have this police officer arrest you for bad debt."

Angelo courteously replied, "Nearly the same amount of money that I owe you is owed to me by Antipholus. Just before I met you, I gave him a necklace that he is going to pay me for at five o'clock. If you would, please walk with me to his house. He will pay me the money he owes me, and I will pay you the money I owe you with my thanks."

Antipholus of Ephesus and Dromio of Ephesus now arrived on the scene, having just left the courtesan.

The police officer saw them and said, "You need not walk to his house. Antipholus has saved you that labor — he is walking toward us now."

Antipholus of Ephesus said to Dromio of Ephesus, "While I go to the goldsmith's house, you go and buy a piece of rope. I will use it to brandish as I shout at my wife and her confederates for locking me out of my own house today. That is the gift I will bestow on her and them. I see the goldsmith. Go, Dromio. Buy a piece of rope and take it to me at my house."

I am buying a thousand pounds a year. I am buying a piece of rope, Dromio thought. *I am being sarcastic, of course. Even if I bought a piece*

39

of rope every day for a year, the weight would not add up to a thousand pounds. I know that my master would not really hurt his wife, so the piece of rope I will buy will be a piece of thin twine that would not hurt even if it were used as a whip instead of as a stage prop. That will save my master money. I, of course, could well receive a thousand poundings from my master — three beatings a day for a year! Ouch! Ouch! Ouch! A smart schoolboy who is sent out to find a branch to be whipped with knows to bring back a twig.

Antipholus of Ephesus said to Angelo, "A man would be well helped if you said that you would help him — ha! I told the courtesan that you would show up for dinner with the necklace, but neither you nor the necklace showed up. Perhaps you thought that you and I would be too friendly if we were chained together, and so you did not come to me with the golden links of the necklace."

"All joking aside, Antipholus, here is the bill for the necklace," Angelo said. "It lists how much your necklace weighs to the exact carat, and it describes the fineness of the necklace's gold and its intricate workmanship. The total cost amounts to three ducats more than I owe to this gentleman. Please, pay him immediately because he is about to go on a voyage and stays here only to receive the money."

"I don't have the money on me," Antipholus of Ephesus said. "Besides, I have some business to take care of in town. Good Signior, take the stranger to my house and take the necklace with you and tell my wife to pay you the sum you have written on the bill. I will try to take care of my business quickly and may be able to return soon enough to see you at my house."

Angelo asked, "Then you will bring the necklace to your wife yourself?"

"No. Take the necklace with you in case I do not quickly arrive."

"Well, sir, I will. Do you have the necklace?"

"If I don't have the necklace, then, sir, I hope you have it. If you don't, you will not get any money from me."

"Please, sir, give me the necklace," Angelo said. "Both wind and tide are waiting for this gentleman, and I am to blame for having held him here so long."

"Good Lord! You are using this tarrying to excuse the breach of your promise to meet me at the Porcupine! I should have criticized you for not bringing the necklace to me there, but like a shrewish man, you were the first to begin to brawl."

The merchant said to Angelo, "The time is passing. Please, sir, pay me."

Angelo said to Antipholus of Ephesus, "You hear how he importunes me for his money. Please give me the necklace!"

"Why, give the necklace to my wife and she will give you your money."

"Come, come, you know I gave the necklace to you just a few minutes ago. Either give me the necklace to give to your wife or give me a note that tells your wife to give me the money."

Antipholus of Ephesus said to Angelo, "You are running this joke into the ground. Where is the necklace? Let me see it, please."

The merchant said to Angelo, "My business is urgent and cannot wait for this delay."

The merchant then said to Antipholus of Ephesus, "Good sir, say whether you'll pay me or not. If you will not, I will have the police officer arrest Angelo."

"I pay you! Why should I pay you!"

Angelo said, "You should pay him the money you owe me for the necklace."

"I don't owe you anything until you deliver the necklace to me."

"You know that I gave you the necklace half an hour ago."

"You did not give me a necklace. You wrong me much when you say that you did."

"You wrong me more, sir, when you say that you did not receive the necklace. Think how this is going to affect my business reputation!"

The merchant said to the police officer, "Well, officer, arrest Angelo the goldsmith for failing to pay his debt."

"I do arrest you, Angelo, and I order you in the Duke's name to obey me."

"This is going to hurt my business reputation," Angelo said to Antipholus of Ephesus. "Either consent to pay this sum for me, or I will have this police officer arrest you for failing to pay your debt."

"You want me to pay for a gold necklace that I never received! Have me arrested, foolish fellow, if you dare."

Angelo said, "Officer, here is the money for your fee to arrest someone for failure to pay his debt. Arrest Antipholus. I would have my own brother arrested if he should treat me so badly and so openly."

"I arrest you, sir," the police officer said. "You have heard the charge made against you."

"I will obey you until I post bail," Antipholus of Ephesus said to the police officer.

He then said to Angelo, "Rascal, you shall pay for this with all the metal in your goldsmith's shop."

"Sir, sir, you will find that the law in Ephesus is on my side. I do not doubt that you will suffer notorious shame."

Dromio of Syracuse returned from the harbor and said to Antipholus of Ephesus, "Master, a ship from Epidamnus is staying at Ephesus only until her owner comes aboard, and then, sir, she sails away. I have carried aboard the ship our baggage, and I have bought the oil, the balm, and the liquor you wanted. The ship is rigged and ready to sail, the merry wind blows in the right direction, and the crew is waiting for their owner, captain, and yourself to board ship so they can set sail."

"What! Are you a madman? Why, you silly sheep, what ship of Epidamnus is waiting for me?"

"The ship you sent me to, to hire passage on it."

"You drunken slave, I sent you to buy a piece of rope, and I told you why I wanted the rope."

"It is just as likely that you sent me to buy a noose so that you can hang yourself," Dromio of Syracuse said. "I repeat, sir, that you sent me to the harbor to find a ship to sail on."

"I will talk to you later about this, and I will teach your ears to listen to me more carefully," Antipholus of Ephesus said. "Go to Adriana, you rascal — hurry and go straight to her. Give her this key, and tell her that in the desk that is covered with Turkish tapestry is a bag filled with ducats. Let her send it to me. Tell her that I have been arrested in the street and I need the money to bail myself out of jail. Go, slave, and hurry!"

He said to the police officer, "Let's go, officer. Take me to prison until I get the bail money."

The merchant, Angelo, the police officer, and Antipholus of Ephesus all exited.

Dromio of Syracuse said to himself, "I must go to Adriana's house, which is where we earlier dined, and where Nell, aka Dowsabel, claimed that I was engaged to be her husband. Dowsabel is my name for her when I am being sarcastic. It is derived from the French *douce et belle* and the Italian *dulcibella*, meaning 'sweet and pretty' or 'sweetheart.'"

Also, the word "dowdy" is derived from the Middle English word *doude*, meaning an *immoral, unattractive, or shabbily dressed woman.*

Dromio of Syracuse concluded, "There I must go, although against my will, for servants must their masters' orders fulfill."

— 4.2 —

In a room in the house of Antipholus of Ephesus, Adriana and Luciana were talking.

"Luciana, did he really try to make you fall in love with him? Could you tell by his eyes whether or not he was serious? Yes or no? How did he look? Red or pale? Serious or merry? What conclusion did you make from watching the changing expressions of his face?"

"First he said that you have no right of him. He said that you and he were not married."

"He meant that he does not live up to his duties as a husband. That is true, and that increases my vexation."

"Then he swore that he was a stranger here."

"That is both truly sworn and falsely sworn. He acts strangely, and yet he is no stranger."

"Then I pleaded on behalf of you."

"And how did he respond?" Adriana asked.

"I begged that he love you, and he begged that I love him."

"With what persuasion did he tempt you to love him?" Adriana asked.

"He used words that might have been persuasive if his had been a honorable courtship. He first praised my beauty and then he praised my speech."

"Did you praise him?" Adriana asked quickly and urgently.

"Be patient, please."

"I cannot and I will not be patient and still. My tongue, although not my heart, shall have what it wants, and my tongue wants to criticize him. He is deformed, crooked, old and sere, ugly, bad bodied, and unshapely everywhere; he is vicious, ungentle, foolish, blunt, and unkind; he is badly deformed in body and worse deformed in mind."

"Who could be jealous then of such a man? No one mourns for an evil when it is gone."

"Yes, but what I think about him is better than what I say about him, and furthermore I wish that other women did not look at him so favorably," Adriana said. "What I say about him and what I think about him are two different things. A lapwing bird builds nests on the ground, and when a predator approaches the nest, the lapwing often pretends to be hurt and hops away on one leg and cries loudly to distract the predator and move it away from the nest. My heart prays for my husband, although my tongue curses him."

Dromio of Syracuse ran up to Adriana and breathlessly exclaimed, "Here! Go! The desk! The bag! Sweetie-pie! Now! Make haste!"

Adriana thought, *It must be important. He is so excited that he called me "Sweetie-pie." That is quite a liberty for a slave to take.*

Luciana asked, "Why are you out of breath?"

"I have been running fast."

"Where is your master, Dromio?" Adriana asked. "Is my husband well?"

"No, he is not well. He is in Tartarus and Limbo, worse than Hell. A Devil in an everlasting garment has him. The Devil is one whose heart is as hard as steel. The Devil is a fiend and a goblin, pitiless and rough. The Devil is a wolf — nay, worse, he is a fellow dressed in a tough and protective leather uniform. The Devil is a 'friend' who creeps up on you from behind. The Devil is a 'friend' who claps you on the shoulder. He is one who knows the passages of alleys, creeks, and narrow lands so that he can track sinners. The Devil is a hunting hound that sometimes goes in the opposite direction that its prey is following, and yet he is a hound that can track sinners well. Sometimes, it is good to know where sinners have been as well as to know where they are going. The Devil who has your husband is one that before Judgment Day carries poor souls to Hell."

"Why, man, what is the matter?"

"I do not know what the specific matter is. My master just told me to come here and get him money for bail."

"What, has he been arrested? Tell me at whose suit he has been arrested."

"It is true that your husband has been arrested by a police officer — a Devil — and is now in prison. I don't know at whose lawsuit he has been arrested, but I can tell you that a policeman who was wearing a protective leather jacket — part of the official uniform of police officers here in Ephesus — arrested him. Will you send your husband, mistress, the money that is in his desk so that he can redeem himself by bailing himself out of jail?"

"Go and fetch it, sister," Adriana said to Luciana, who took the key from Dromio and left to get the money.

Adriana said, "My husband is a businessman and must have been arrested for bad debt, but I wonder how he could be in debt without my knowing about it. Tell me. Was he arrested because of a legal bond?"

Even in an emergency, Dromio of Syracuse willfully misunderstood words. "Was he arrested because of a linen band of cloth? No. He was arrested because of something much stronger. Something that has links like a chain. He was arrested because of a necklace. Listen! Can you hear it ring?"

"Hear the links of the necklace ring? Don't you mean jangle?"

"No, I just heard the bell of a clock. It is time that I was gone. It was two o'clock before I left my master, and the clock just struck one."

"Is time running backward? I have never heard of that happening before."

"Oh, yes, it does happen to hours. When an owe-er — someone who looks at all his debt and says 'ow' and so is an ow-er — who cannot pay his debts sees a police officer ahead of him, he runs back the way he came. And of course it is illegal to be a woman who is paid to cry 'Oh! Oh! Oh!' Therefore, when an oh-er or a 'ho-er sees a police officer in front of her, she runs back the way she came. Both are afraid of being arrested."

"Time running back the way it came! As if Time were in debt! How foolishly you think!"

"Time is a bankrupt, and he owes more than he's worth. We never have enough Time to accomplish what we want to accomplish in any season. Indeed, Time is a thief, too. Haven't you heard men say that Time comes stealing on by night and day? If Time is a bankrupt and a thief, and a police sergeant appears in Time's way, doesn't Time have a reason to turn back like an owe-er or an ow-er or an oh-er or a 'ho-er every day?"

Luciana returned with the money for bail.

"Go, Dromio," Adriana said. "There's the money; carry it straight to my husband and bring him home immediately."

She said to Luciana, "Come, sister. What I am imagining is too much for me. What I am imagining causes me both pleasure and pain. I imagine the comfort that my husband will get when he is bailed out of jail, but I also remember the way that my husband has been treating me."

<h3 align="center">— 4.3 —</h3>

Antipholus of Syracuse, who was wearing the necklace that Angelo the goldsmith had given to him, stood on a public street and said to himself, "Every man I meet here in Ephesus greets me as if I were his very good friend. Every man calls me by my name. Some give money to me; some invite me to dinner; some give thanks to me for kindnesses; some offer to sell me commodities. Just now a tailor called me into his shop and showed me silks that he said he had bought for me and then he took my measurements. Surely these are tricks of my imagination, and surely sorcerers who were educated in Lapland, that country of magic, live here."

Dromio of Syracuse walked up to Antipholus of Syracuse and said, "Master, here's the gold you sent me for. What, have you gotten redemption from the picture of old Adam in his new apparel?"

Dromio of Syracuse thought, *Odd. My master seems not only to have bailed himself out of jail without the money to do it with, but he also has acquired a new gold necklace. Has the police officer suddenly turned super-friendly?*

"What gold is this? And what Adam do you mean?"

"I don't mean that Adam who kept the Garden of Eden, but I do mean that Adam who keeps the prison.

"The Adam I mean wears leather — the skin of the calf that the father ordered to be killed for the Prodigal Son. The Prodigal Son's father was happy to see his son and had the fatted calf killed to provide a feast to celebrate his son's return, but the Adam I mean wears a police officer's leather uniform and arrests prodigals who cannot pay their debts. Of course, the first Adam's first clothing was made of fig leaves, but both Adams later wore animal skins for clothing. Remember Genesis 3:21: 'Unto Adam also and to his wife did the LORD God make coats of skins, and clothed them.'

"The Adam I mean is the one who came from behind you, sir, like an evil angel, and made you forsake your liberty.

"The Adam I mean is the opposite of the good angel who released Paul from prison in Acts 12:5-7: 'So Peter was kept in the prison, but prayer for him was being made fervently by the church to God. On the very night when Herod was about to bring him forward, Peter was sleeping between two soldiers, bound with two chains, and guards in front of the door were watching over the prison. And behold, an angel of the Lord suddenly appeared and a light shone in the cell; and he struck Peter's side and woke him up, saying, 'Get up quickly.' And his chains fell off his hands.'"

"I have no idea what you are talking about."

"You don't? Why, I am speaking plainly about a plain case. I am talking about the man who walks around looking like the musical instrument called a bass that is still in its leather case. This man, sir, who is dressed in a leather uniform, when gentlemen are tired, gives them a reason to sob and arrests them and lets them rest in prison. He, sir, takes pity on bankrupt men who cannot afford new clothing and gives them new suits — suits of law, aka lawsuits. I am talking about a man who while making an arrest does more damage with his nightstick than a soldier does with his bayonet."

"Are you talking about a police officer?"

"Yes, sir, I am talking about the sergeant of the band, the man who brings a man to court to answer for breaking his bond. This sergeant apparently thinks that men are always going to bed, and therefore often says, 'God give you good rest!' But actually he is always thinking about good arrests that will stand up in courts."

"That is a good place for you to rest and stop your joking. Are any ships leaving Ephesus tonight? Can we set sail tonight?"

"Why, sir, I brought you word an hour ago that the ship *Expedition* is setting sail tonight. Unfortunately, you were then arrested by the police officer and so were forced to wait for the ship *Delay*. By the way, here are the angels — the gold coins — that you sent me to get so that you could pay your bail."

"You are confused in your mind, and so am I. Here in Ephesus, we wander around in illusions of our mind. May some blessed power deliver us from here!"

The courtesan walked over to them and said, "Well met, Master Antipholus. I see, sir, from the necklace that you are wearing that you have seen the goldsmith who failed to show up for dinner and bring the necklace to you — that is why you left before we enjoyed our after-dinner dessert. I assume that this is the necklace that you promised to give me."

Antipholus of Syracuse had never seen the courtesan before and so he thought that she was a figure of evil: one of the many witches reputed to live in Ephesus. He said, "Satan, avoid! I charge thee, tempt me not," using some of the words of Jesus as they appeared in the 1599 Geneva Bible: "Then said Jesus unto him, 'Avoid[,] Satan: for it is written, Thou shalt worship the Lord thy God, and him only shalt thou serve'" (Matthew 4:10).

"Avoid, Satan" was another way of saying, "Get away from me, Satan" or "Depart, Satan" or "Get lost, Satan."

Dromio of Syracuse asked, "Master, is this person Mistress Satan?"

"She is the Devil."

"No, she is worse," Dromio of Syracuse said. "She is the Devil's dam, aka the Devil's mother. She has appeared here in front of us dressed like a woman with loose — or nonexistent — morals. In other words, she looks like a cheap date. Sometimes, women say, 'God damn me!' That is the same thing as saying, 'God, make me a cheap date' or 'God, make me a dam, aka mother.' It is written that Devils sometimes appear to men like angels of light: 'And no marvel, for Satan himself is transformed into an angel of light' (2 Corinthians 11:14). Light is an effect of fire, and fire will burn; ergo, cheap dates will burn — they will give men a venereal disease that will make the men burn when they pee. Do not go near her, master. On second thought, she looks like she might be a very expensive 'date.'"

"Your slave and you are very funny, sir," the courtesan said. "Will you go with me? Shall we enjoy our after-dinner dessert here in my house?"

"Master, if you do go and eat with her, expect to use a spoon to eat soft food, such as children and old people use to eat with, for you would have to be simple-minded to eat with such a woman as this. If you do go and eat with her, make sure that you use a spoon with a long handle."

"Why, Dromio?"

"Whoever wants to eat with the Devil must have a long spoon."

Antipholus of Syracuse said to the courtesan, "Avoid, fiend! Get lost! Why are you talking to me about after-dinner dessert? You are, like everyone else here in Ephesus, either a sorceress or magician. I conjure you to leave me and be gone."

"We made a trade at dinner: I gave you a diamond ring and you promised to give me a gold necklace. Give me the ring of mine you had at dinner, or, in exchange for my ring, give me the necklace you promised to give to me, and I'll be gone, sir, and not trouble you."

As the courtesan had said, Antipholus of Ephesus and she had made a trade at dinner: She had given him her diamond ring worth forty ducats, and in return he had promised to give her a gold necklace worth two hundred ducats. If the courtesan was unable to get the necklace, she wanted to at least get her ring back.

Dromio of Syracuse said, "Some Devils ask for only the parings of one's fingernails, a straw, a hair, a drop of blood, a pin, a nut, a cherry pit, or other items that can be used in making potions or casting spells, but this female Devil, who is greedier, wants to have a necklace. Master, be wise: Do not give her the necklace. For if you give it to her, the Devil will shake the links of the necklace like the links of a chain and frighten us with it. Remember Revelation 20:1-2: 'And I saw an angel come down from Heaven, having the key of the bottomless pit and a great chain in his hand. And he laid hold on the dragon, that old serpent, which is the Devil, and Satan, and bound him a thousand years.'"

"Please, sir," the courtesan said. "Give me my ring back, or else give me the necklace. I hope that you do not intend to cheat me."

"Avaunt, you witch!" Antipholus of Syracuse said. "Get away from me, you witch!"

"Avaunt" means "go away" or "get lost."

Then he added, "Come, Dromio, let us go."

Dromio of Syracuse said, "A courtesan accusing us of cheating is like a peacock with its ornate feathers accusing someone of being proud. Mistress, you know all about that. Pride is one of the seven deadly sins, and it is personified by a whore — the citizens of Babylon were proud, and the whore of Babylon had something written on her forehead: 'And upon her forehead was a name written, MYSTERY, BABYLON THE GREAT, THE MOTHER OF HARLOTS AND ABOMINATIONS OF THE EARTH'" (Revelation 17:4).

Antipholus of Syracuse and Dromio of Syracuse exited, leaving behind the courtesan, who said to herself, "It must be that Antipholus is insane, or he would never behave in this way. He has a ring of mine that is worth forty ducats, and for that ring he promised me a necklace. Now he refuses to give me either the ring or the necklace. The reason why I think that he is insane, besides the way he was acting just now, is the wacky story he told me today at dinner: He said that his own door was shut and locked so that he could not enter his home. Apparently, his wife, knowing about his fits of insanity, purposely locked the door to keep him from entering the house. Now I need to go to his home and tell his wife a lie. I will say that her husband, who is a lunatic, rushed into my house and took away my ring from me by force. This course of action is the best that I can choose because forty ducats is too much for me to lose."

— 4.4 —

On a street of Ephesus stood Antipholus of Ephesus and the police officer.

"Don't be afraid, officer," Antipholus of Ephesus said. "I will not try to run away. I'll give you, before I leave you, as much money as is needed to bail me out of jail. My wife is in a wayward mood today, and she will not easily believe a messenger who gives her the news that I have been arrested in Ephesus. That unwelcome news will, I tell you, sound harshly in her ears."

Dromio of Ephesus arrived, carrying the piece of rope that he had been sent to buy.

Antipholus of Ephesus said to the police officer, "Here comes my man; I think he brings the money needed to bail me out of jail."

He called, "Now, sir! Have you gotten what I sent you for?"

"Here's something that, I warrant you, will pay them all back for the way they treated you," Dromio of Ephesus said, holding the piece of rope: a thin, limp piece of twine.

"But where's the money?"

"Why, sir, I paid the money for the rope."

"You paid five hundred ducats, rascal, for a rope?"

"I will give you five hundred ropes in return for five hundred ducats."

"To what end or purpose did I order you to hurry home?"

52

"To get a piece of rope, sir — the rope's end, and having accomplished that purpose I have returned."

"I intended to use that piece of rope as a stage prop to hold as I threaten my wife," Antipholus of Ephesus said, looking at the thin, limp piece of twine that Dromio of Ephesus had brought to him.

He added, "And to my purpose for that end of rope, sir, I welcome you," and he started hitting Dromio of Ephesus with the thin, limp piece of twine.

"Good sir, calm down," the police officer said to Antipholus of Ephesus.

"Why don't you tell me to be patient?" Dromio of Ephesus said. "I am the one who is suffering adversity! Remember what the Prayer Book version of Psalm 94:13 says: 'That thou mayest give him patience in time of adversity.'"

"Be good, now," the police officer said. "Hold your tongue."

"It would be better if you told him to hold his hands still," Dromio of Ephesus, who was still being hit with the twine, said.

Antipholus of Ephesus said, "You son of a whore! You senseless rascal!"

"I wish I were without senses, sir — especially the sense of touch. That way, I would not feel your blows."

Of course, the blows from the twine did not hurt. Dromio of Ephesus simply liked to complain.

"You are sensible in — that is, you understand — nothing but blows, and so you are like an ass."

"I am an ass, indeed," Dromio of Ephesus said. "You may prove it by looking at my long ears."

He said to the police officer, "Indeed, I have served my master for many long years — from the hour of my nativity to this instant, and I have had nothing at his hands for my service but blows. When I am cold, he heats me by beating me. When I am warm, he cools me by beating me. I am awakened from sleep by being beaten. When I sit,

I am ordered to stand up by being beaten. When I need to leave our home, I am driven from it by being beaten. When I return home, I am welcomed by being beaten. I bear my beatings on my shoulders the way that a beggar woman bears her brat. Someday, one of his beatings will make me lame, and then I will be a beggar who limps from door to door."

Antipholus of Ephesus said, "Come, let's go and meet my wife, who I see is walking toward us with some other people."

Adriana, Luciana, and the courtesan walked toward Antipholus of Ephesus, Dromio of Ephesus, and the police officer. With them was a man called Pinch because of his pinched face. He had the reputation of being a learned conjuror, although he did not use Latin in his exorcisms.

Dromio of Ephesus said to Adriana, "Mistress, *respice finem*, which is Latin for 'respect your end.' Or, better, *respice funem*, which is Latin for 'respect your rope.' Beware of having your end come at the end of a rope; for many people, at the end of the rope is a noose. You have heard parrots that have been taught to say 'rope.' By the way, have you noticed that your husband has the end of a rope?"

"Are you still blabbing!" Antipholus of Ephesus said, using his hat to hit Dromio of Ephesus.

"What do you think now?" the courtesan asked Adriana. "Don't you think that your husband is mad?"

Adriana replied, "His incivility and terrible behavior confirm no less."

She then said, "Good Doctor Pinch, you are a conjurer. Get my husband back in his right senses, and I will give you whatever you will demand."

Luciana said, "It's sad. How fiery and sharp and angry he looks!"

"Look how he trembles in his frenzy!" the courtesan said. "He has been possessed by a malevolent spirit."

Pinch said to Antipholus of Ephesus, "Give me your hand and let me feel your pulse."

Antipholus of Ephesus replied, "Here is my hand, and let it feel your ear."

He hit Pinch on the ear.

Pinch attempted an exorcism: "I order you, Satan, who is housed within this man, to leave this man's body as ordered by my holy prayers and to hurry home to the pit of darkness. I exorcise you with the help of all the saints in Heaven!"

"Shut up, you doting and doddering wizard, shut up! I am not mad," Antipholus of Ephesus said.

"I wish that you weren't, you poor distressed soul!" Adriana said.

Antipholus of Ephesus said to her, "You loose woman, you hussy, are these your customers? Did this companion with the yellow pinched face revel and feast at my house today while you shut and locked the door to prevent me from entering my own house?"

"Husband, God knows that you ate dinner at home. I wish that you had stayed at home until now — you would have avoided all this trouble and gossip and shame and embarrassment!"

"You say that I dined at home!" Antipholus of Ephesus said to his wife.

He asked Dromio of Ephesus, "Rascal, what do you say about that?"

"Sir, you did not dine at home, and that is the truth."

"Isn't it true that my door was shut and locked so that I could not enter my own house?" Antipholus of Ephesus asked.

"It is true that your doors were locked and you were shut out of your own house."

"Is it true that my wife insulted me after locking me out of my house?" Antipholus of Ephesus asked.

"Yes, your wife insulted you after locking you out of your house."

"Didn't her kitchen-maid rail at, taunt, and scorn me?" Antipholus of Ephesus asked.

"Yes, she did; the kitchen-vestal who keeps the fire going scorned you."

"Didn't I depart from there in a rage?" Antipholus of Ephesus asked.

"Truly, you did depart in a rage. My bones bear witness that you departed in a rage because they have felt the depth of your rage."

Adriana asked Pinch, "Is it a good idea to pretend to agree with my mad husband when he says such crazy things?"

"There is no shame in it," Pinch replied. "This slave has figured out that agreeing with his master is a good way to keep him from being violent."

Antipholus of Ephesus said to Adriana, "You convinced the goldsmith to have me arrested."

She replied, "I gave Dromio money to take to you so that you could bail yourself out of jail when he came here and urgently asked for it."

"Gave me money!" Dromio of Ephesus said. "She might have given me heart and goodwill and her best wishes, but as for money, she gave me not even a farthing, master."

Antipholus of Ephesus asked him, "Didn't you go to her and ask her to give you a bag full of gold ducats so you could bring it to me?"

Adriana said, "He came to me and asked me for it, and I gave it to him."

Luciana added, "And I witnessed her doing it."

"May God and the rope maker bear witness that I was sent to get nothing but a piece of rope!" Dromio of Ephesus said.

"Mistress, both the slave and his master are possessed by malevolent spirits — I can tell by their pale and deadly looks," Pinch said. "They must be bound and laid in some dark room."

Antipholus of Ephesus asked his wife, "Adriana, why did you lock me out of my own home?"

He asked Dromio of Ephesus, "And why didn't you give me the bag full of gold ducats?"

Adriana replied, "I did not, gentle husband, lock you out of your own home."

Dromio of Ephesus replied, "And, gentle master, I received no gold. But I acknowledge, sir, that we were locked out of the house."

Adriana said to Dromio of Ephesus, "You lying rascal. You lied twice just now."

Antipholus of Ephesus said to his wife, "Adriana, you lying harlot, you have lied in everything you said. You have plotted with a damned pack of scoundrels to mock me and make me a laughingstock. But with my fingernails I will pluck out your false eyes that want to see me mocked and shamed!"

Adriana screamed, and three or four men came and tried to tie up Antipholus of Ephesus, who fought them.

Adriana said, "Tie him up! Tie him up! Don't let him come near me!"

Pinch shouted, "We need more help! The fiend possessing him is powerful!"

"The poor man!" Luciana said. "How pale and wan he looks!"

Finally tied up, Antipholus of Ephesus shouted, "What, are you trying to murder me? Police officer, I am your prisoner. Are you going to allow them to take me from you?"

The police officer said, "Let him go. He is my prisoner, and you shall not have him."

Pinch pointed to Dromio of Ephesus and said, "Tie up this man because he is also possessed by a malevolent spirit."

Men tied up Dromio of Ephesus.

Adriana asked, "What are you doing, you silly police officer? Do you take pleasure in seeing a wretched man do outrage and harm to himself?"

"He is my prisoner," the police officer said. "If I let him go, I will be required to pay the debt he owes."

Adriana replied, "I will pay the debt before I leave you. Take me to my husband's creditor. Once I know what the debt is and I am satisfied that it is genuine, I will pay it."

She said to Pinch, "Good master doctor, see my husband safely conveyed home to my house. This is a very unhappy day!"

"You are a very unhappy strumpet!" Antipholus of Ephesus said to his wife.

"Master, I have been tied up and bound to you because of you," Dromio of Ephesus said.

Antipholus of Ephesus replied, "Rascal, why are you enraging me!"

"Why should you be bound for nothing?" Dromio of Ephesus asked. "Since they think that you are insane, you should act as if you are insane. Shout, 'The Devil!' Let them think that you are talking to the Devil that is supposed to be possessing you."

"May God help these poor souls," Luciana said. "How crazily they talk!"

"Take my husband and his slave to our home," Adriana said.

She then said, "Sister, come with me. We will go with this police officer."

Everyone left except for Adriana, Luciana, the police officer, and the courtesan.

Adriana asked the police officer, "Who charged my husband with not paying his debt and got him arrested?"

"Angelo, a goldsmith. Do you know him?"

"I know the man. What is the sum my husband owes?"

"Two hundred ducats."

"For what is it owed?"

"Your husband ordered and received a gold necklace."

"My husband ordered a gold necklace to be made for me, but as far as I know, he never received it."

The courtesan said, "I told you earlier that your husband in a fit of insanity came to my house today and carried away my ring — I saw him wearing my ring just now. Just after he carried away my ring, I saw him on the street wearing a gold necklace."

"That may be true, but I have never seen the necklace," Adriana said. "Come, police officer, take me to the goldsmith. I want to learn the truth about what is going on."

Antipholus of Syracuse and Dromio of Syracuse entered the scene. Because Antipholus of Syracuse was afraid of the witches and warlocks with whom Ephesus seemed to be infested, he had drawn his sword and made Dromio of Syracuse draw his dagger.

Seeing them, Luciana cried, "May God have mercy! Your husband and his slave have gotten loose!"

Adriana said, "And they are brandishing weapons. Let's call for more help to have them tied up again."

The police officer cried, "Let's run away — or they'll kill us!"

Everyone ran away, leaving Antipholus of Syracuse and Dromio of Syracuse behind by themselves.

Antipholus of Syracuse said, "I see that these witches are afraid of swords."

"The woman who called herself your wife ran away," Dromio of Syracuse said.

"Let's go to the Centaur Inn and fetch our baggage from there. I wish that we were safe and sound on board a ship quickly sailing away from Ephesus."

"Let's stay here tonight," Dromio of Syracuse said. "The inhabitants will surely not do us harm. You have seen that they are afraid of weapons and that they speak kindly to us and that they have given gold to us. I think that Ephesus is a town filled with good people, and except for the mountain of mad flesh who claims to be engaged to marry me, I could find it in my heart to stay here always and become a warlock."

"I would not stay here tonight even if doing so would get me all the possessions of the entire town. Therefore, let's go and get our baggage and carry it on board ship."

CHAPTER 5

— 5.1 —

Angelo the goldsmith and the merchant to whom he owed money stood on a street in front of an abbey, aka nunnery.

"I am sorry, sir, that I have hindered you from starting your travels," Angelo said, "but I swear that Antipholus received the necklace from me, although he very dishonestly denies it."

"What is his reputation here in Ephesus?"

"He is very well regarded, sir. He receives infinite credit from businesspeople, he is highly beloved, and he is second to none who live here in the town. On the basis of his word alone, I would lend him my entire net worth."

He thought, *Or I would have until today — he must not be in his right mind now.*

"Speak softly. I think that is him walking over there."

Antipholus of Syracuse and Dromio of Syracuse walked toward them. Antipholus of Syracuse was still wearing the gold necklace around his neck.

"That is him," Angelo said, "and he is wearing around his neck the gold necklace we were talking about although he swore to the police officer that he had not received it. Good merchant, sir, draw nearer to me so that you can support me. I'll speak to him."

Angelo then said, "Signior Antipholus, I wonder much that you would put me to this shame and trouble, and not without some scandal to yourself. You swore to the police officer that you had not received the gold necklace, but now I see that you are openly wearing it around your neck. In addition to being legally charged with not paying your debt, as well as suffering shame and imprisonment, you have done wrong to this man, who is my honest friend. He would have hoisted sail and put to sea today except that he had to stay here because of the controversy

61

revolving around the necklace. Can you now deny having received that necklace from me?"

"I did receive this necklace from you. I know that I have never denied receiving this necklace from you."

The merchant, who had been a witness, said, "Yes, you did deny receiving the necklace from Angelo, sir, and you swore to the police officer that you did not receive the necklace from Angelo."

"Oh, really? And who has ever heard me deny receiving the necklace or swear that I never received it?"

"These ears of mine heard it," the merchant said. "You know that they heard it. Shame on you, wretch! It is a pity that you are allowed to walk on the streets alongside honest men."

"You are a villain to accuse and slander me in this way. I'll prove that I am an honorable and honest man to you right now, if you dare to draw your sword and stand against me."

"I do dare to draw my sword, and I do call you a villain."

Both Antipholus of Syracuse and the merchant drew their swords. Angelo the goldsmith did not.

Adriana, Luciana, the courtesan, and a few other people arrived on the scene.

"Stop!" Adriana said. "Don't hurt my husband, for God's sake! He is insane. Some of you get inside his guard and take his sword away. Tie up Dromio, too, and take them to my house."

Dromio of Syracuse said, "Run, master, run. For God's sake, find a place we can take refuge in. Look, here is an abbey. Let us find sanctuary here, or we are ruined!"

Antipholus of Syracuse and Dromio of Syracuse ran inside the abbey.

The Abbess, who was named Emilia, walked out of the abbey and said, "Be quiet, people. Why are you thronging around the abbey gate?"

"We want to fetch my poor mentally disturbed husband from here," Adriana said. "Let us come in so that we may tie him up securely and take him home so he can recover from his madness."

"I knew that he could not be in his right mind," Angelo said to the merchant.

"I am sorry now that I drew my sword against him," the merchant replied.

"How long has madness possessed him?" the Abbess asked.

"This week he has been heavy in spirits, sour, melancholy, and much different from the man he used to be," Adriana said, "but not until this afternoon did his sickness make him violently angry."

"What is the reason for his madness? Has he lost a lot of wealth because of a shipwreck? Has he buried a dear friend? Has he fallen in love with another woman? That is a sin that is very common in youthful men who allow their eyes to wander. Which of these sorrowful things have happened to him?" the Abbess asked.

"None of these, except the last one," Adriana said, glancing at the courtesan. "He has some other woman who draws him away from home."

The Abbess thought, *I will attempt to find out the cause of this man's madness by questioning his wife. I will see how she has been treating — or mistreating — him. Because she suspects that he has been unfaithful to her, she may have been shrewish and too badly mistreated him. We must find a mean between extremes. Not enough of something is bad. Too much of something is bad. Exactly the right amount is good.*

"If he leaves home to see another woman, you should criticize him for that," the Abbess said.

"Why, so I have," Adriana said.

"Yes, but not roughly enough," the Abbess said.

"As roughly as my modesty would let me," Adriana said.

"Perhaps you criticized him only in private," the Abbess said.

"In private, yes, but in public, too," Adriana said.

"Yes, but you did not criticize him strongly enough," the Abbess said.

"It was the only topic of our conversation," Adriana said. "In bed I did not allow him to sleep because I kept talking about it. At meals I did not allow him to eat because I kept talking about it. When we were alone together, it was the only topic I talked about. When we were in the company of other people, I often mentioned it. Always, and over and over, I told him that what he had done was vile and bad."

"And because of your shrewishness, this man went mad," the Abbess said. "The venomous clamors of a jealous woman are a poison more deadly than the poison that comes from the bite of a mad dog. Based on what you just told me, it seems your railing at him hindered his sleep, and therefore his head is now disoriented. You said that you seasoned his food with your upbraidings: Clamorous meals have as a consequence poor digestion, from which comes the raging fire of fever. What is a fever but a fit of madness? You said that his entertainments were marred by your brawls.

"Unless one engages occasionally in sweet recreations, one suffers moody and dull melancholy, which is related to grim and comfortless despair, and at the heels of despair follow a huge infectious troop of pale illnesses and foes to life. You have disturbed his life-preserving rest, his meals, and his sweet entertainments. When that happens to any man or beast, the result is madness.

"Based on what you have told me, I have concluded that your jealous fits have driven from your husband his ability to use his wits."

Luciana defended her sister: "Adriana never reprehended him except mildly and gently, while he behaved in a rough, rude, and wild manner."

She asked her sister, "Why do you bear these rebukes? Why don't you defend yourself?"

"The Abbess is right," Adriana replied. "She said the things necessary for me to see that I was wrong."

She then said, "Good people, enter the abbey and lay hold of my husband and carry him out."

"No, I will not allow any person to enter the abbey," the Abbess said.

"Then let your servants bring my husband out."

"No. He entered my house in order to get sanctuary, and he will get it. As long as he is in the abbey, he is beyond the reach of the law. He shall be protected from being taken away by your hands until I have brought him to his wits again, or tried to bring him back to his wits but failed."

Adriana said, "I will look after my husband and be his nurse and feed him healthy food. This is my duty as his wife, and I will have no one else but me do it. He is my husband in sickness and in health; therefore, let me take my husband home with me."

"Be patient and stay calm," the Abbess said. "I will not allow him to leave here until after I have used the tried and tested means I have of restoring him to health: wholesome syrups, medicinal drugs, and holy prayers. This will make him a formal — a well-formed, aka normal — man again. It is a part and parcel of my oath — it is a charitable duty of my religious order. Therefore, depart and leave him here with me."

"I will not go away and leave my husband here," Adriana said. "It ill suits your holiness to separate a husband and a wife."

"Be quiet and depart. You shall not take him away from here."

The Abbess went inside the abbey.

Luciana advised her sister, "Complain to the Duke of Ephesus about this indignity."

"Yes, I will fall prostrate at his feet and never rise until my tears and prayers have persuaded his Grace to come in person here and take away by force my husband from the Abbess."

The merchant said, "By this time, I think, the shadow cast by the sundial points at five — it is five o'clock. Soon, I am sure, the Duke himself in person will come this way to the melancholy vale — the place of death and sorrow-causing execution — behind the drainage ditches of the abbey here. Such is the news that I have heard today."

Angelo asked, "Why is the Duke going there today?"

"To see an old merchant from Syracuse, who unluckily put into this bay against the laws and statutes of this town. He will be beheaded publicly for his offence."

"Look, the Duke and the old merchant are coming," Angelo said. "We will witness the old merchant's death."

Luciana said to Adriana, "Kneel to the Duke before he passes the abbey."

Duke Solinus, accompanied by his attendants, and Egeon, the old merchant from Syracuse, now arrived. The Headsman — the executioner — and other officers also arrived. Egeon was bareheaded in readiness for his beheading.

Duke Solinus said, "Yet once again proclaim it publicly that if any friend will pay the ransom for this respectable old merchant, then the old merchant shall not die. We value and respect him that much."

Adriana knelt and said loudly, "Give me justice, most sacred Duke, against the Abbess!"

Duke Solinus said, "The Abbess is a virtuous and a reverend lady: It cannot be that she has done wrong to you."

Adriana replied, "May it please your Grace, I am concerned about Antipholus, my husband, whom I made Lord of me and all I had, with your approval as shown by your letters in support of him.

"This ill day, a most outrageous fit of madness took him with the result that desperately he hurried through the street. His slave, who was as insane as my husband, went with him. They annoyed the citizens of Ephesus by rushing into their houses and taking away rings, jewels, and anything that my husband in his madness wanted. I was able for a time to have my husband tied up and sent home, while I attempted to make amends for the wrongs he had committed here and there in his madness.

"Very quickly, and I do not know how he did it, he escaped from the men who were guarding him, and he and his insane slave, each extremely angry, with drawn swords, met us again and madly attacked us, and chased us away until, after raising more help, we came again to tie them up. Then they fled into this abbey, where we pursued them. And here the Abbess shuts the gate against us and will not allow us to fetch my husband out, nor will she send him out so that we may take him away from here.

"Therefore, most gracious Duke, command that my husband be brought out of the abbey and taken to his home so that he may receive help for his madness."

Duke Solinus said, "Long ago your husband served me in my wars, and when you married him and made him master of your bed, I promised — giving my word as Prince — to do him all the grace and good I could."

The Duke then ordered, "Go, some of you, knock at the abbey's gate and order the Abbess to come to me. I will settle this matter before I leave here."

One of Adriana's servants arrived and said to her, "Oh, mistress, mistress, run away and save yourself! My master, Antipholus, and his man, Dromio, have both broken loose. They have beaten the maids one after the other and tied up Doctor Pinch. They have singed his beard off with brands of fire, and as it burned, they threw on him great pails of muddy water from puddles to quench his burning hair. My master, Antipholus, mocks Doctor Pinch by telling him to stay calm and carry on, and all the while his man Dromio uses scissors to give Doctor Pinch the haircut of a fool. Surely, unless you immediately send some help, between them they will kill Pinch the conjurer."

"Be quiet, fool! Your master and his man are here in the abbey, and everything that you have said is false."

"Mistress, I swear upon my life that I am telling you the truth. I have almost not had time to breath since I witnessed it. Your husband cries for you, and he vows that when he finds you he will smear charcoal all over your face and so disfigure you."

Some cries sounded.

The servant continued, "Listen! I hear him, mistress. Run away! Go now!"

Duke Solinus said, "Come, stand by me, Adriana and Luciana; fear nothing. Guards, be ready to use your weapons!"

"It is my husband!" Adriana said. "All of you are witnesses that my husband can do impossible things. He travels about invisibly. Just now we had him trapped in the abbey here, but now he is over there. Human reason cannot explain how that happened. The abbey has high walls around it and only one gate: the one in front of us."

Antipholus of Ephesus and Dromio of Ephesus ran over to the group of people.

Antipholus of Ephesus said, "Give me justice, most gracious Duke. Give me justice! Remember the service that long ago I did for you when I stood over you in the wars and suffered deep scars in order to save your life. In return for the blood that I shed then to save your life, grant me justice now."

Egeon thought, *Unless the fear of death is making me imagine things, I see Antipholus, my son, and Dromio, his slave.*

Antipholus of Ephesus said, "Give me justice, sweet Prince, against that woman there! She is the woman whom you gave to me to be my wife. She has abused and dishonored me in the most egregious ways possible! Beyond imagination is the wrong that she this day has shamelessly done to me."

"Tell me what has happened, and you will find that I am just and fair," Duke Solinus said.

"On this day, great Duke, she shut and locked the door of my house so that I could not get in, while she with people of low character feasted in my house."

"That would be a grievous fault!" Duke Solinus said.

He asked Adriana, "Tell me, woman, did you do what your husband says you did?"

"No, my good Lord. Three of us — I myself, my husband, and my sister — today dined together. I swear on my soul that what my husband said is not true!"

Luciana said, "May I never stay awake during the day, nor sleep at night, if what my sister is telling your Highness is not the simple truth!"

Angelo the goldsmith thought, *That is perjury! Both women lied! In this instance, the madman is telling the truth and justly making charges against them!*

Antipholus of Ephesus said, "My Liege, I am in my right mind and I know what I am saying. I am neither drunk and disturbed with the effect of wine, nor am I heady-rash and provoked with raging ire, although the wrongs that I have endured might make someone wiser than I insane.

"This woman locked me out of my house today and kept me from eating dinner there. That goldsmith there, if he were not in league with her, could bear witness to what I say, for he was with me then. He departed from me to go and fetch a necklace, promising to bring it to the Porcupine, where Balthazar and I dined together. Our dinner done, and the goldsmith not coming to the Porcupine, I went to seek him.

"In the street I met him, and in his company was that gentleman, a visiting merchant. Also with them was a police officer. At that time this goldsmith perjured himself by swearing that I this day received the necklace from him — the necklace that, God knows, I have never seen. The goldsmith then had the police officer arrest me. I obeyed the orders of the police officer, and I sent my slave home to get a bag of ducats so I could post bail. My slave returned with no ducats. Then I politely spoke to the officer and asked him to go in person with me to my house.

"On our way there, we met my wife, her sister, and a rabble consisting of her vile confederates. Along with them they brought a man named Pinch, who is a hungry, lean-faced villain; a mere skeleton;

a mountebank; a threadbare magician and a fortune-teller; a needy, hollow-eyed, sharp-looking wretch; a dead-looking man. This pernicious slave pretended to be a conjurer, and he gazed into my eyes and felt my pulse. He was so scrawny that he seemed to have no face, but he disconcerted me by staring steadily at me. He cried out that I was possessed.

"Then all together they fell upon me, tied me up, carried me away from there, and left me and my slave, both of us bound together, in a dark and dank room with an arched ceiling at home. Eventually I was able to use my teeth to gnaw in two the ropes binding us. I gained my freedom, and I immediately ran here to see your Grace, whom I beseech to give me ample satisfaction for these deep shames and great indignities."

Angelo said, "I can in part vouch for the madman's story. I know for a fact that he did not dine at home, and I know for a fact that he was locked out of his house."

Duke Solinus asked, "Did he receive a necklace from you, or not?"

"He did, my Lord. People here saw that he was wearing the necklace when he ran into the abbey just now."

The merchant said to Antipholus of Ephesus, "In addition, I will swear that these ears of mine heard you confess that you had received the necklace from Angelo although you had earlier sworn in the marketplace that you had not received it. When I said that you had earlier sworn that you had not received the necklace, we quarreled and drew our swords, and then you fled into this abbey here, from whence, I think, you have come by a miracle."

Antipholus of Ephesus said, "I have never been inside the walls of this abbey, and you have never drawn a sword against me. In addition, I have never seen the necklace, so help me, Heaven! Most of the things you are saying about me are false."

"Why, what an intricate case this is!" Duke Solinus said. "I think you all have drunk a potion from the cup of the pagan goddess Circe and been enchanted. If all of you had really driven Antipholus into this abbey, he would still be there. If he were really mad, he would not be able to speak so rationally. Adriana says that he dined at home; Angelo the goldsmith denies that."

Duke Solinus turned to Dromio of Ephesus and asked, "What have you got to say about this?"

Dromio of Ephesus pointed to the courtesan and replied, "Sir, Antipholus dined with this woman at the Porcupine."

The courtesan said, "He did, and from my finger snatched that ring he is wearing."

Antipholus of Ephesus said, "It is true that I received this ring from her."

Duke Solinus asked the courtesan, "Did you see him enter the abbey here?"

"Yes, as surely and as clearly, my Liege, as I see your Grace."

"Why, this is strange," Duke Solinus said.

He turned and ordered one of his men, "Go tell the Abbess to come out here."

The man left to go and get the Abbess.

Duke Solinus then said, "I think that all of you are either confused or stark mad."

Egeon, who had been quiet, now said, "Most mighty Duke, give me permission to speak a few words. Perhaps I see a friend here who will save my life and pay the sum that may deliver me from execution."

"Speak freely, man of Syracuse. Say whatever you wish."

Egeon asked, "Isn't your name, sir, Antipholus? And isn't that man your bondman, aka slave, Dromio?"

Dromio of Ephesus replied, "Within this hour I was his bondman, sir — he and I were bonded, aka bound, together. But he, and I thank him for it, gnawed in two the bonds that bound me. Now am I Dromio and his man, aka slave, unbound."

Egeon said, "I am sure that both of you remember me."

"By looking at you, we remember in what situation we were recently, sir. For lately we were bound and tied up, as you are now. Are you one of Pinch's patients, sir?"

"Why do you look at me as if you do not know me?" Egeon asked. "You know me well."

Antipholus of Ephesus replied, "I have never seen you in my entire life until now."

Egeon said, "Grief has changed me since you saw me last, and hours filled with cares have used time's deforming hand to write wrinkles on my face. But please tell me, don't you recognize my voice?"

"No," Antipholus of Ephesus said.

Egeon asked, "How about you, Dromio?"

"No. Trust me, sir, I do not."

"I am sure that both of you do," Egeon said.

Dromio of Ephesus said, "I am sure I do not, and whatever a man denies, you who are bound are bound to believe him."

"Not know my voice!" Egeon said. "Time, you who are so very severe, have you so cracked and split my poor tongue in seven short years, that now my only son does not know my feeble key of untuned cares? My voice is like unmelodious music, and my song describes my sorrows. Although this lined face of mine is now hidden by winter's drizzled snow that stops tree sap from circulating — that is, my white beard — and although all my veins have frozen my blood and made it cold, yet my night of life, aka old age, has some memory left, my wasting lamps that are my eyes have some fading glimmer left, and my dull and deaf ears are still able to hear a little. All these old witnesses tell me that you are my son Antipholus. I cannot be wrong about that."

Antipholus of Ephesus said, "I have never seen my father in my life."

Upset, Egeon said, "You know that it has been only seven years since we parted in Syracuse, boy."

He hesitated and then said, "But perhaps, my son, you are ashamed to acknowledge that I am your father because I am a prisoner."

Antipholus of Ephesus said, "You come from Syracuse, and the Duke and all who know me in this town can bear witness that I have never seen Syracuse in all my life."

Duke Solinus said, "I can tell you, merchant of Syracuse, that for twenty years I have been the patron of Antipholus, during which time he has never seen Syracuse. I see that your old age and the danger you are in are making you talk foolishly."

Emilia now walked up to Duke Solinus, bringing with her Antipholus of Syracuse and Dromio of Syracuse.

She said, "Most mighty Duke, behold a man who has been much wronged."

The two Antipholuses stood side by side, and the two Dromios stood side by side.

Everyone stared at them.

Adriana said, "I see two husbands, or my eyes deceive me."

Duke Solinus looked at the two Antipholuses and said, "One of these men must be the genius — the attendant spirit that follows him throughout his life and looks exactly like him — of the other."

He looked at the two Dromios and said, "The same is true of these two other men."

He then asked of both sets of men, "Who is the natural man, and who is the attending spirit? Who can tell the difference?"

Dromio of Syracuse said, "I, sir, am Dromio; command the spirit who looks exactly like me to go away."

Dromio of Ephesus said, "I, sir, am Dromio; please, let me stay."

Antipholus of Syracuse said to his father, "Are you Egeon? Or are you his ghost?"

Dromio of Syracuse looked at Egeon and said, "It is my old master! Who has tied him up?"

Emilia said, "No matter who bound this man, I will loosen this man's bonds and gain a husband by his liberty. Speak, old Egeon, if you are the man who once had a wife named Emilia who bore to you in one birth two beautiful sons. If you are that same Egeon, speak, and speak to the same Emilia, who is me!"

"Unless I am dreaming, you really are Emilia," Egeon said. "If you are she, tell me what happened to that son who floated away with you on the fatal raft?"

"He and I and the twin Dromio were all rescued by men of Epidamnus, but by and by violent fishermen of Corinth used force to take Dromio and my son away from me. They took my son away and left me with the men of Epidamnus. What then happened to my son and his slave, I cannot tell. I eventually arrived at this fortune that you see me in."

Duke Solinus thought, *Why, here we see that the story that the old merchant of Syracuse told me this morning is true. Look at these two Antipholuses; these two are entirely alike. And look at these two Dromios; they are the same in appearance. The merchant of Syracuse told me about the wreck at sea, and I now know that Egeon and Emilia are the parents to these children, who by accident have finally met.*

He asked one of the Antipholuses, "Antipholus, did you come originally from Corinth?"

Antipholus of Syracuse replied, "No, sir, not I; I came from Syracuse."

Duke Solinus said to the two Antipholuses, "Stand a little distance apart from each other; I do not know which of you is which."

Antipholus of Ephesus said, "I came originally from Corinth, my most gracious Lord —"

Dromio of Ephesus said, "And I came with him."

Antipholus of Ephesus said, "We were brought to this town by that most famous warrior, Duke Menaphon, your most renowned uncle."

Adriana asked, "Which of you two dined with me today?"

Antipholus of Syracuse replied, "I did, gentle mistress."

"Are you my husband?"

Antipholus of Ephesus said, "He is not. I can most emphatically say that."

Antipholus of Syracuse said, "I can confirm that I am not married to Adriana, although she said that I was her husband. And this fair gentlewoman, her sister here, called me brother."

He said to Luciana, "What I told you then, when we were alone after dinner, I hope I shall have leisure to make good, if this is not a dream that I see and hear."

Angelo said, "That is the necklace, sir, which you received from me."

Antipholus of Syracuse said, "It is, sir. I do not deny it."

Antipholus of Ephesus said to Angelo, "And you, sir, had me arrested because of this necklace."

Angelo replied, "I think I did, sir. I do not deny it."

Antipholus of Syracuse handed the necklace to Antipholus of Ephesus, who hung it around the neck of his wife, Adriana.

Adriana said to her husband, "I sent money to you, sir, to be your bail. Dromio was supposed to give you the money, but I think he did not bring it."

Dromio of Ephesus said, "No money was sent by me."

Antipholus of Syracuse said, "I received the bag of ducats you sent, Adriana, and Dromio of Syracuse, my slave, brought them to me. I see that my brother and I met each other's slave, and I see that I was mistaken for my brother, and he for me, and thereupon these errors arose."

Antipholus of Syracuse gave the bag of gold ducats to his brother, Antipholus of Ephesus.

Antipholus of Ephesus said, "With these ducats I pay the ransom for my father here."

"You need not do that," Duke Solinus said. "I hereby pardon your father without ransom and allow him to live."

The courtesan said to Antipholus of Ephesus, who was wearing her ring, "Sir, I must have that diamond ring that you are wearing; it is mine."

Antipholus of Ephesus took off the ring and gave it to the courtesan, saying, "Here, take it; and thank you very much for entertaining me."

Emilia said, "Renowned Duke, please go with us into the abbey here and hear all of us tell our stories. If anyone here has suffered any wrong from the mishaps of this day, come and keep us company, and we shall make everything right. For thirty-three years, it has been as if I have labored to give birth to you, my twin sons, and until this hour right now I did not give birth. Now I am able to see and enjoy my two sons. The Duke, my husband, and my twin children, and you two Dromios, who are the calendars of my twins' nativity, having been born in the same hour and on the same day as them, go into the abbey and enjoy the feast that celebrates a birth or baptism. After enduring grief for so long, it is time to enjoy festivity!"

Duke Solinus said, "With all my heart, I'll celebrate and enjoy this feast."

Emilia cut the bonds of Egeon, and hand in hand they walked into the abbey.

Everyone exited except for the two Antipholuses and the two Dromios and Adriana and Luciana.

Dromio of Syracuse said, "Master, shall I fetch your baggage from the ship?"

Antipholus of Ephesus asked, "Dromio, what baggage of mine have you put on board a ship?"

"All of your belongings that were at the Centaur Inn, sir."

Antipholus of Syracuse said to Antipholus of Ephesus, "He thought he was talking to me."

Antipholus of Syracuse said to Dromio of Syracuse, "I am your master, Dromio. Come and go with us. We'll take care of the baggage later. Embrace your brother there; rejoice with him."

The two Antipholuses went inside the abbey. Antipholus of Ephesus went in while holding hands with Adriana, his wife. Antipholus of Syracuse went in while holding hands with Luciana, Adriana's sister.

Dromio of Syracuse said to his brother, "A fat friend at your master's house thought that I was you and entertained me in the kitchen during dinner today. She now shall be my sister, not my wife."

"I think that you are my mirror, and not my brother," Dromio of Ephesus replied. "I see by you that I am a sweet-faced youth. Will you go into the abbey with me and see the celebration?"

"I will not go in ahead of you, sir. You are the older brother, so you should go in first."

"Am I the older brother? We don't know for sure. How shall we decide who is older?"

"Let's draw straws. Until then, you will enjoy the rights of the older brother."

Dromio of Ephesus said, "No. Instead, let's do this. We came into the world brother and brother, so now let's go into the abbey hand in hand, and not one before the other."

Dromio of Syracuse and Dromio of Ephesus held hands and walked into the abbey together.

APPENDIX A: ABOUT THE AUTHOR

It was a dark and stormy night. Suddenly a cry rang out, and on a hot summer night in 1954, Josephine, wife of Carl Bruce, gave birth to a boy — me. Unfortunately, this young married couple allowed Reuben Saturday, Josephine's brother, to name their first-born. Reuben, aka "The Joker," decided that Bruce was a nice name, so he decided to name me Bruce Bruce. I have gone by my middle name — David — ever since.

Being named Bruce David Bruce hasn't been all bad. Bank tellers remember me very quickly, so I don't often have to show an ID. It can be fun in charades, also. When I was a counselor as a teenager at Camp Echoing Hills in Warsaw, Ohio, a fellow counselor gave the signs for "sounds like" and "two words," then she pointed to a bruise on her leg twice. Bruise Bruise? Oh yeah, Bruce Bruce is the answer!

Uncle Reuben, by the way, gave me a haircut when I was in kindergarten. He cut my hair short and shaved a small bald spot on the back of my head. My mother wouldn't let me go to school until the bald spot grew out again.

Of all my brothers and sisters (six in all), I am the only transplant to Athens, Ohio. I was born in Newark, Ohio, and have lived all around Southeastern Ohio. However, I moved to Athens to go to Ohio University and have never left.

At Ohio U, I never could make up my mind whether to major in English or Philosophy, so I got a bachelor's degree with a double major in both areas, then I added a master's degree in English and a master's degree in Philosophy.

Currently, and for a long time to come (I eat fruits and vegetables), I am spending my retirement writing books such as *Nadia Comaneci: Perfect 10*, *The Funniest People in Dance*, *Homer's* Iliad: *A Retelling in Prose*, and *William Shakespeare's* Macbeth: *A Retelling in Prose*.

By the way, my sister Brenda Kennedy writes romances such as *A New Beginning* and *Shattered Dreams*.

APPENDIX B: SOME BOOKS BY DAVID BRUCE

Retellings of a Classic Work of Literature

Arden of Faversham: A Retelling

Ben Jonson's The Alchemist: A Retelling

Ben Jonson's The Arraignment, or Poetaster: A Retelling

Ben Jonson's Bartholomew Fair: A Retelling

Ben Jonson's The Case is Altered: A Retelling

Ben Jonson's Catiline's Conspiracy: A Retelling

Ben Jonson's The Devil is an Ass: A Retelling

Ben Jonson's Epicene: A Retelling

Ben Jonson's Every Man in His Humor: A Retelling

Ben Jonson's Every Man Out of His Humor: A Retelling

Ben Jonson's The Fountain of Self-Love, or Cynthia's Revels: A Retelling

Ben Jonson's The Magnetic Lady, or Humors Reconciled: A Retelling

Ben Jonson's The New Inn, or The Light Heart: A Retelling

Ben Jonson's Sejanus' Fall: A Retelling

Ben Jonson's The Staple of News: A Retelling

Ben Jonson's A Tale of a Tub: A Retelling

Ben Jonson's Volpone, or the Fox: A Retelling

Christopher Marlowe's Complete Plays: Retellings

Christopher Marlowe's Dido, Queen of Carthage: A Retelling

Christopher Marlowe's Doctor Faustus: Retellings of the 1604 A-Text and of the 1616 B-Text

Christopher Marlowe's Edward II: A Retelling

Christopher Marlowe's The Massacre at Paris: A Retelling

Christopher Marlowe's The Rich Jew of Malta: A Retelling

Christopher Marlowe's Tamburlaine, Parts 1 and 2: Retellings

Dante's Divine Comedy: A Retelling in Prose

Dante's Inferno: A Retelling in Prose

Dante's Purgatory: A Retelling in Prose

Dante's Paradise: A Retelling in Prose

The Famous Victories of Henry V: A Retelling

From the Iliad to the Odyssey: A Retelling in Prose of Quintus of Smyrna's Posthomerica

George Chapman, Ben Jonson, and John Marston's Eastward Ho! A Retelling

George Peele's The Arraignment of Paris: A Retelling

George Peele's The Battle of Alcazar: A Retelling

George Peele's David and Bathsheba, and the Tragedy of Absalom: A Retelling

George Peele's Edward I: A Retelling

George Peele's The Old Wives' Tale: A Retelling

George-a-Greene: A Retelling

The History of King Leir: A Retelling

Homer's Iliad: A Retelling in Prose

Homer's Odyssey: A Retelling in Prose

J.W. Gent.'s The Valiant Scot: A Retelling

Jason and the Argonauts: A Retelling in Prose of Apollonius of Rhodes' Argonautica

John Ford: Eight Plays Translated into Modern English

John Ford's The Broken Heart: A Retelling

John Ford's The Fancies, Chaste and Noble: A Retelling

John Ford's The Lady's Trial: A Retelling

John Ford's The Lover's Melancholy: A Retelling

John Ford's Love's Sacrifice: A Retelling

John Ford's Perkin Warbeck: A Retelling

John Ford's The Queen: A Retelling

John Ford's 'Tis Pity She's a Whore: A Retelling

John Lyly's Campaspe: A Retelling

John Lyly's Endymion, The Man in the Moon: A Retelling

John Lyly's Galatea: A Retelling

John Lyly's Love's Metamorphosis: A Retelling

John Lyly's Midas: A Retelling

John Lyly's Mother Bombie: A Retelling

John Lyly's Sappho and Phao: A Retelling

John Lyly's The Woman in the Moon: A Retelling

John Webster's The White Devil: A Retelling

King Edward III: A Retelling

Mankind: A Medieval Morality Play (A Retelling)

Margaret Cavendish's The Unnatural Tragedy: A Retelling

The Merry Devil of Edmonton: A Retelling

The Summoning of Everyman: A Medieval Morality Play (A Retelling)

Robert Greene's Friar Bacon and Friar Bungay: A Retelling

The Taming of a Shrew: A Retelling

Tarlton's Jests: A Retelling

Thomas Middleton's A Chaste Maid in Cheapside: A Retelling

Thomas Middleton's Women Beware Women: A Retelling

Thomas Middleton and Thomas Dekker's The Roaring Girl: A Retelling

Thomas Middleton and William Rowley's The Changeling: A Retelling

The Trojan War and Its Aftermath: Four Ancient Epic Poems

Virgil's Aeneid: A Retelling in Prose

William Shakespeare's 5 Late Romances: Retellings in Prose

William Shakespeare's 10 Histories: Retellings in Prose

William Shakespeare's 11 Tragedies: Retellings in Prose

William Shakespeare's 12 Comedies: Retellings in Prose

William Shakespeare's 38 Plays: Retellings in Prose

William Shakespeare's 1 Henry IV, aka Henry IV, Part 1: A Retelling in Prose

William Shakespeare's 2 Henry IV, aka Henry IV, Part 2: A Retelling in Prose

William Shakespeare's 1 Henry VI, aka Henry VI, Part 1: A Retelling in Prose

William Shakespeare's 2 Henry VI, aka Henry VI, Part 2: A Retelling in Prose

William Shakespeare's 3 Henry VI, aka Henry VI, Part 3: A Retelling in Prose

William Shakespeare's All's Well that Ends Well: A Retelling in Prose

William Shakespeare's Antony and Cleopatra: A Retelling in Prose

William Shakespeare's As You Like It: A Retelling in Prose

William Shakespeare's The Comedy of Errors: A Retelling in Prose

William Shakespeare's Coriolanus: A Retelling in Prose

William Shakespeare's Cymbeline: A Retelling in Prose

William Shakespeare's Hamlet: A Retelling in Prose

William Shakespeare's Henry V: A Retelling in Prose

William Shakespeare's Henry VIII: A Retelling in Prose

William Shakespeare's Julius Caesar: A Retelling in Prose

William Shakespeare's King John: A Retelling in Prose

William Shakespeare's King Lear: A Retelling in Prose

William Shakespeare's Love's Labor's Lost: A Retelling in Prose

William Shakespeare's Macbeth: A Retelling in Prose

William Shakespeare's Measure for Measure: A Retelling in Prose

William Shakespeare's The Merchant of Venice: A Retelling in Prose

William Shakespeare's The Merry Wives of Windsor: A Retelling in Prose

William Shakespeare's A Midsummer Night's Dream: A Retelling in Prose

William Shakespeare's Much Ado About Nothing: A Retelling in Prose

William Shakespeare's Othello: A Retelling in Prose

William Shakespeare's Pericles, Prince of Tyre: A Retelling in Prose

William Shakespeare's Richard II: A Retelling in Prose

William Shakespeare's Richard III: A Retelling in Prose

William Shakespeare's Romeo and Juliet: A Retelling in Prose

William Shakespeare's The Taming of the Shrew: A Retelling in Prose

William Shakespeare's The Tempest: A Retelling in Prose
William Shakespeare's Timon of Athens: A Retelling in Prose
William Shakespeare's Titus Andronicus: A Retelling in Prose
William Shakespeare's Troilus and Cressida: A Retelling in Prose
William Shakespeare's Twelfth Night: A Retelling in Prose
William Shakespeare's The Two Gentlemen of Verona: A Retelling in Prose
William Shakespeare's The Two Noble Kinsmen: A Retelling in Prose
William Shakespeare's The Winter's Tale: A Retelling in Prose